Bayard's mission in life is simple: fight against the conclave and protect humanity and supernatural creatures alike. To do that, he and the other heroes who left the conclave need the help of everyone they can convince, including heroes who still believe the conclave is doing the right thing like Percival.

Percival was captured by the fallen heroes and is sitting in a cell. It's admittedly a nice cell, but Percival has no intention of joining the fallen heroes.

When Percival's siren half surfaces, Percival panics. He can't go back to a conclave that would kill him if they found out about it, but he still believes in the conclave's mission to protect humanity. There's no place for him with the conclave, but is there one with the fallen heroes?

Bayard wants Percival to see the truth about the conclave, and he hopes to do that by linking them together using a spell. They can't be apart while the spell is active, but can they learn to live together? Or will Percival run back to the conclave as soon as he finds a way?

Like Truth
Copyright © 2021 Catherine Lievens
ISBN: 978-1-4874-3363-5
Cover art by Angela Waters

Published by eXtasy Books Inc

Look for us online at:
www.eXtasybooks.com

LIKE TRUTH
VIKINGS 5

BY

CATHERINE LIEVENS

CHAPTER ONE

Bayard glared at the screen. He understood why this job was necessary, but was he really the one who had to do it? "There are too many of them," he complained.

"Which is why the three of us are doing this," Mordred said from further down the table. "I could have asked you to do it on your own."

Bayard groaned and turned his attention back to his computer. "There are more than a hundred messages here."

"I'll take the first thirty. You take the next thirty. Eudocia will take another thirty."

"What about the last ones?"

Mordred shrugged. "We'll see once we get there."

And new emails were arriving as Bayard stared at the screen. This was going to be a long day.

With a sigh, he opened the first message. It only took him a few moments to realize he didn't need to read it to know what the hero who'd sent it wanted. It was full of insults and threats, so Bayard clicked out of it and moved it to a new folder. He labeled it *idiots we need to look into* and moved on to the next email.

"What's that folder supposed to mean?" Eudocia asked. She sounded amused.

"Open it and check the email I put there. You'll see."

Bayard could hear her click around, so he waited. She snorted, then made a disgusted sound.

"You know, I think I knew this guy when I was still with the conclave. He *is* an idiot," she said.

"It's a good idea to keep threatening emails," Mordred added. "At least we know who we're never going to be able to convince of the truth."

Unfortunately, they all knew that some heroes would stay with the conclave. For some, it was because they were idiots who couldn't see what the conclave was doing. For others, it was because they knew what the conclave was doing, and they didn't care. Some of them no doubt agreed with killing all supernatural creatures and were eager to do their jobs. Unfortunately, being a hero didn't mean you were a good person.

Just like Bayard had expected, this was hard work. After the third email, he'd already had enough of threats. He also wanted to find the idiots who had written those emails and beat them into the ground, but instead, he limited himself to moving the emails to the folder he'd created earlier and moving on to the next one.

Luckily, he found a few hesitant emails asking for more information about what the conclave was doing. Those he moved to a folder Mordred had created. They would have to contact the heroes who'd written them later so they could give them more information and make sure they weren't spies.

The door creaking open made the three of them look up. Eudocia waved at Amyas, then turned her attention back to her screen, but Bayard could already do with a break, so he leaned back in his chair and watched. Amyas walked in and made a beeline for Mordred. He sat in the seat next to his boyfriend and leaned close to him. Their shoulders brushed together for a moment before Mordred wrapped an arm around Amyas's waist and pulled him even closer, almost in his lap. Amyas chuckled but didn't protest.

Bayard swallowed. He was happy Mordred and Amyas had found each other. They both deserved happiness, and he didn't care that it meant Mordred was a bit distracted or had better things to do instead of working all the time. It meant more work for Bayard, but it wasn't like he had anyone waiting for him in his room anyway. Mordred did now, and he should spend as much time with Amyas as he could.

All of them were immortal unless someone beheaded them or something equally dramatic. But they were warriors, which meant they could die any day. Mordred himself went out on missions as often as he could, and he could get hurt, or worse. Bayard would do everything he could to make sure that didn't happen, but he'd lost friends over the decades, and it would happen again. There was nothing he could do about it, unfortunately.

"You're staring," Eudocia said.

She hadn't even looked away from her screen, but she was smiling.

Bayard considered telling her she was wrong, but she knew him too well. They'd been friends for hundreds of years, and she was one of the people he was closest to. "I don't understand how you're not. Don't you want what they have?" he asked in a whisper.

She finally looked at him. "I don't know. It looks sweet, but also like a lot of work."

Bayard pressed his lips together so he wouldn't laugh. "Even then. They finally have someone to share the next decades with." Being immortal had its perks, but it also had its downfalls. It was lonely, even when you managed to find someone to share your life with.

Bayard had had a few relationships, most of them with other heroes, but unfortunately, they hadn't worked out. They hadn't been the right people, to the point that he wondered if the right person was still out there for him. Maybe he was, and he just needed to wait and see what happened. Mordred was much older than he was, and he'd only just now found Amyas. Bayard had to keep his mind open, and of course, his eyes.

Was what Mordred and Amyas had something he even wanted? Right now, it sounded good, but he knew himself. He felt lonely, so he wanted a relationship. That didn't mean he'd look for someone or that he'd look the other way if he met the right person, but he felt as if his life was on pause. The only thing he could focus on was his job, so after one last glance at Mordred and Amyas, who were quietly talking while Amyas pointed at the screen, he went back to work.

He had a lot to be grateful for, even without a special person in his life. He was immortal, something a lot of humans and supernatural creatures would kill for. He had a home, friends, and people he considered his family, even though they weren't related by blood. All of those were things not many other heroes had, and that was one of the reasons he was never going back to the conclave.

The conclave was evil, as far as Bayard was concerned. They killed supernatural creatures just because of what they were, something they couldn't change. It wasn't the only bad thing they did. They took teenagers and children from their homes, and they were never allowed to go back. Just because they had the hero mark, it made them the conclave's property. The conclave raised them to be warriors and tried to beat emotions out of them.

Heroes weren't allowed to have relationships, especially not with another hero. They weren't allowed to go against the conclave or even to doubt the orders they were given. The only thing they could do was obey, and that was easier to do if they didn't think. Bayard had done that for a long time, but that was in the past. Now, he was doing the right thing, and no matter how hard it was, he'd never go back. He was free of the conclave, free to disobey orders to kill innocent beings, and free to have his own family.

Sooner or later, he'd find a special someone like Mordred

had. When he did, he'd protect them from the conclave and the heroes who worked for them. In the meantime, he'd focus on the job and try to convince as many heroes as possible to leave the conclave. Even if they weren't willing to work with Mordred and Bayard, they wouldn't be going around killing innocent beings, and that was all Bayard wanted.

Percival stared at the wall. There was nothing else for him to do, since he was in a cell.

He hated himself for being captured, although he'd been unconscious when it happened. The reason he'd been unconscious was that he'd tried to take on Mordred, and he'd lost. This was his punishment, and unfortunately, he knew the conclave wasn't coming for him.

They weren't that kind of organization. They lost heroes every day, but they never looked back. They couldn't afford to, not with the work they had to do. Instead, they continued recruiting new heroes.

All of that meant that if Percival wanted out of the cell, he was going to have to do it on his own. The problem was that he had no idea how.

He had to admit he hadn't been treated badly, not like he'd expected to be. He'd seen enough heroes and supernatural creatures imprisoned by the conclave. They tortured their prisoners to get the answers they needed, and once they had those, they killed the prisoners. That was what Percival had expected from the fallen heroes. Instead, they'd stuck him in a cell, and he'd been there ever since.

And what a cell it was. It was nothing like the damp and dark rooms at the conclave. It was still a cell, and there was no denying that. There were no windows, and the door was locked. It had a tiny opening so Percival could look into the hallway when he wanted, but he'd realized early on there wasn't anything interesting to look at unless someone was coming to him.

That was where the cell aspects of the room he was in ended. It was comfortable—even more comfortable than his room with the conclave. There, he only had a bed with a hard and thin mattress, and a dresser. He had to share a bathroom with dozens of other heroes. There was no privacy, and while he wanted out of this place, the comfort was the one aspect he'd miss.

The cell had a bathroom, and it was walled off so no one could see him from the hallway while he was in there. He'd been puzzled in the beginning, because it was a dangerous thing not to be able to see your prisoner anytime you needed to, but he'd realized the fallen heroes weren't afraid of him or what he could come up with. Every time he'd tried to escape, they'd stopped him. Why would they be afraid?

The bed in the cell was comfortable and much bigger than the one he was used to. There was a dresser, and he'd been given clothes and toiletries. There was also a TV, and the shelves lining one of the walls were heavy with books. If it weren't for the fact that Percival couldn't leave the place, it would almost be like a vacation.

That was why he didn't know what to think about any of this. The only thing he was sure of was that he couldn't trust the fallen heroes.

They'd left the conclave. They went against conclave orders to kill supernatural creatures. Percival had been with the conclave for a long time, and if they gave that order, they had a good reason to. Going against that would endanger both heroes and humans, and that wasn't something he could allow.

He also couldn't allow doubt to tinge his thoughts.

At the sound of footsteps coming closer, he sat up in his bed. The TV was on, and he turned it off, but he already knew what was about to happen. It was lunchtime, which meant one of his jailers was bringing him food.

If Percival had been a conclave prisoner, he'd have been lucky to be given some water and a piece of bread. Here, he had a full meal three times a day. It was becoming a problem, since he didn't have the space to train, but he'd been doing what he could to keep up with his training and not lose too much muscle. No one had told him he couldn't, so he spent part of his morning and afternoon doing just that.

The sound of beeping brought his attention back to the door. Initially, he'd hoped it had a key he might be able to steal from his captors, but it didn't. It opened through a code, and only his jailers knew it. No matter how many times he tried to watch when they punched it in, he hadn't been successful. He also suspected they changed it at least once a day, possibly more often. Even if he got the code, he wouldn't be able to do anything with it.

The door swung open. Percival almost groaned when Constantine walked in. All of the jailers were friendly enough and tried to talk to him, but Constantine was the worst. He didn't seem to care that Percival glared and growled at him. He continued chatting as if they were best friends, and he never hesitated to sit on the edge of Percival's bed and keep him company while he was eating, no matter how many times Percival told him he didn't need or want him to.

Constantine grinned. "Good morning."

Percival glared. He'd tried everything with Constantine—ignoring him, telling him to fuck off, even trying to kill him. Nothing worked. Constantine kept being friendly, and Percival didn't know how to deal with him.

Constantine was holding a tray. He closed the door behind himself with his foot, then moved into the room to put the tray on the small table in the corner. Because that was something else Percival had—the only thing he was missing was a couch, and he'd have a full apartment. Unfortunately for him, there were two chairs at the table, which meant Constantine sat in one of them.

They'd already gone through this plenty of times since Percival had awakened in his cell. Ignoring Constantine wouldn't work, and neither would staying away from him or refusing to eat.

Percival got to his feet and headed to the bathroom to wash his hands. When he came back, Constantine was stealing baby carrots from his plate. Percival growled as he sat in the empty chair, but it wasn't enough for Constantine to stop. Instead, he shrugged.

"I put more carrots on your plate so we could share," he said, snatching another one. It crunched when he bit into it.

Percival looked at his plate. Whoever had gotten his food ready — probably Constantine — had made him a massive sandwich with chicken, lettuce, tomatoes, and mayo. Next to it on the tray was a bowl of baby carrots and a second bowl full of crackers. Constantine had added a bottle of water, although Percival had plenty of that in his cell.

Percival's stomach growled. He ignored Constantine's stare and picked up the sandwich, giving it a bite.

It was good. Everything was good, and Percival kept waiting for the other shoe to drop. There was no way the fallen heroes would keep him like this forever. He was still trying to understand what they were attempting to do, but he couldn't come up with anything. He didn't have any conclave secrets to tell them. Most of them had been heroes much longer than he had, and he wasn't stupid enough to think they didn't have spies in the conclave. There was nothing he could give them that they didn't already know, so why was he still here? Why hadn't they killed him?

Because no matter what they kept saying, they were traitors. They'd betrayed the conclave and the heroes. No matter how friendly they were, Percival had to remember that.

"So, what have you been up to?" Constantine asked.

Percival ignored him and gave his sandwich another bite. Unfortunately, that didn't seem to be a problem for Constantine, who continued talking.

"We've been getting a lot of emails after that message Mordred sent. I'm not part of the team going through them, but I know that lots of them are full of insults and threats." He snorted. "I just don't get it. Why can't you even consider that the conclave isn't perfect?"

Percival huffed and tried to focus on his food. He wasn't going to answer that question.

He wasn't sure he could.

Bayard leaned back in his chair. He raised his arms to stretch, grimacing at the sound his neck made when he tilted his head from side to side.

"It's time for a break," Mordred said.

Bayard snorted. "Was it the sound of my bones creaking that made you think that?"

"In part."

And no doubt the other part was due to Amyas, who was still there. He and Mordred had been becoming more and more affectionate as the time passed, and Bayard had no doubt they'd find the nearest closet to disappear into for a quickie. The thought made him grimace, but he couldn't berate them. He'd probably do the same thing if he were in their position.

"The three of you need to eat," Amyas said. "I'm going to the kitchen. I'll bring the food back here, but if you want to step out, feel free to. I'll fetch you when I get back."

Bayard blinked at Amyas's retreating back. "Where is he going?" he asked.

"Didn't you hear him? He said he would fetch us food,"

Mordred answered.

"I did hear him, but I didn't think that was why we'd stopped."

Mordred arched a brow. "Why did you think we stopped, then?"

"So you could fuck him in the closet."

Mordred gaped, while Eudocia sounded like she might die of laughter. She was half draped over the table, tears in her eyes as she howled.

"I wouldn't fuck him in the closet," Mordred said with a growl.

Bayard raised his hands. "Sorry. The two of you have been all lovey-dovey for the past hour, so I thought that was what you had in mind. And don't let our presence stop you. We don't mind if you slip out for a bit."

Eudocia snorted. "As long as what you do isn't obvious. I don't want the room to smell of sex for the rest of the day."

Mordred growled. "I will *not* fuck Amyas in a closet. He deserves more."

Bayard agreed with that. Amyas wasn't a hero, but it didn't mean he hadn't been through a lot. His parents and his tribe had betrayed him, and while he'd found a new family with the heroes, that betrayal wasn't easy to forget. Besides, he was a living being, and that was enough reason to treat him with respect. "Take him to your room, then," he suggested.

"Who's taking who to their room?" Amyas asked as he walked in again, carrying a tray.

"How were you so quick?" Bayard asked. He got to his feet to help Amyas since the tray looked heavy.

"I got all of this ready before coming here an hour ago. I knew the three of you would forget to eat, so I wanted to have everything ready when it was time."

Bayard took the tray from Amyas's hands and put it on the table. He was hungry, but like Amyas had said, he'd probably have forgotten to eat if it weren't for Amyas. There was too much to do and not enough time to do it.

The four of them sat closer to each other so they could all reach the tray. It was heavy with sandwiches and vegetables, and Bayard felt better once he started nibbling on carrots and cucumbers. He was halfway through his first sandwich when Amyas asked, "How's Percival doing?"

That got Bayard's attention. Percival was the latest of Mordred's projects. For the past few decades, Mordred had been kidnapping heroes, locking them in cells in the basement, and convincing them to leave the conclave and work with the fallen heroes instead. With most, it eventually worked. With others, it didn't, and they had to execute those. It wasn't something Bayard or anyone else did with a light heart, but it was necessary. If they couldn't convince the heroes to be on their side, it meant those heroes would be against them eventually if they set them free. They couldn't afford that, no matter how much it hurt to kill.

Mordred sighed. "Honestly, I haven't had enough time to take care of him. The four I've assigned as guards have been doing a good job, but he's not budging. He's still convinced the conclave knows what they're doing and can do no wrong, and I'm getting worried."

Amyas patted Mordred's knee. "But you just said you haven't had a lot of time to be with him. I'm sure that once you find time, you'll convince him."

Mordred and Bayard looked at each other. Bayard knew what Mordred was thinking. The longer Percival was there with no one changing his mind, the harder it would become. It might even become too hard, and Mordred would have to get rid of Percival.

Bayard was surprised Amyas cared. After all, Percival had been one of the heroes who had tried to attack Amyas's tribe. Bayard hadn't been there, but he'd heard both from Mordred and Amyas that Percival had been rude. That wasn't a surprise. Amyas was a supernatural creature, while Mordred was a fallen hero. Percival didn't respect either of them, and things had probably not gotten easier now that he was a prisoner.

"I'll take care of it," he said before he could think better of it.

Everyone else around the table turned to look at him. "Are you offering to talk to Percival instead of me?" Mordred asked. He sounded like he didn't quite believe it, and for a good reason. This wasn't something Bayard usually did. He was on board with trying to change heroes' minds, but he didn't have the patience Mordred had. The few times he'd tried, he'd almost come to blows with the prisoners, and that was never a good thing—especially not when you were trying to convince them to pass to your side.

Bayard bit off half a carrot and gave himself time to chew and swallow before answering. "Why not?"

Eudocia snorted. "Why not? How about why yes? We both know you're not made for this kind of job. Remember the last time you tried?"

Bayard winced. He did remember it. The hero he'd been trying to convince had attacked him, and Mordred and Eudocia had needed to separate them. There had been blood, and a lot of it, not all coming from the prisoner.

"It was a long time ago," Bayard said. "I can do better now."

Bayard didn't know what had pushed him to volunteer, but now that he had, he didn't think it was a bad idea. It would give him a distraction, and maybe he'd stop obsessing over the fact that he didn't have anyone like Amyas in his life. Even though he knew he had all the time in the world to find a special someone, watching Mordred and Amyas together made him jealous and yearn for it to happen now. Working with Percival would hopefully help him stop obsessing over that and let things happen in their own time. Besides, it gave him a good reason to step away from the computers and emails he'd been reading, so it couldn't be a bad idea.

"All right," Mordred said.

Eudocia made a strangled sound. "Really? You're going to trust him with that?"

Mordred shrugged. "I trust him with my life. Why not this?"

"They're going to kill each other."

"If they do, I expect Bayard to win." Mordred looked at Bayard. "But you've watched me do this enough times. You know what to do. Don't let him get to you, and I'm sure you'll get the results we need."

And that was to convince Percival to move to their side. Now that Bayard really thought about it, maybe volunteering wasn't such a good idea. How was he supposed to convince a hero who hated his guts to become his friend?

But he'd never spoken to Percival. The hero had been put in one of the cells in the basement as soon as he'd arrived, and he'd still been unconscious. Since then, only the four guards assigned to him had walked into his cell. If Bayard wanted to do this, the first step would be talking to Percival and see how bad the situation was. Once he knew, he could decide what the next step would be.

Percival waited until Constantine was out the door to rush toward it. He tried to get there in time to be able to stick his hand or his foot through so Constantine wouldn't be able to close it, but the only thing he managed was to get Constantine to open the door again and stare at him.

"That was kind of pathetic," Constantine said.

Percival glared at him. "I'd like to see you in my place."

"I was, once."

The words were enough to give Percival pause. "What do you mean?"

"Exactly what I said. I *was* in your place once. Or did you think I was always a fallen hero? Just like everyone else here, I worked for the conclave. I was captured and brought here, and Mordred convinced me to change sides. In fact, I used to live in this very cell."

Percival looked around. He'd known there was no way he was the first to stay here, but Constantine? He looked so much at ease working against the conclave, and he'd told Percival so many things about the fallen heroes that Percival hadn't even thought about the fact that he'd once worked for the conclave. "How could Mordred convince you this was the right thing to do?" he asked.

Constantine shrugged. "You'll realize it, too, eventually. Mordred is convincing."

"I haven't seen him yet."

Constantine grimaced. "Yeah, he's been really busy, what with the conclave trying to kill him and everything. I'm sure he'll come around. He always does, and he's managed to convince almost all the heroes we captured over the decades."

"What happens to those he can't convince?"

Constantine didn't have to answer for Percival to know. His expression was enough.

"But that won't happen to you," Constantine said.

Percival crossed his arms over his chest. "You can't know that. I'm a conclave hero, and that's never going to change. What you people are doing isn't right. We were created to protect humanity, and you're going against that."

Constantine sighed. "I thought you'd gotten over that, but I guess I was wrong. You really should try to make more of an effort if you want to break free, though."

Percival cringed. "I'll manage next time."

"Sure. Isn't that what you said the last time you tried?"

It was, and now Percival wanted to strangle Constantine. He might even try if he didn't know Constantine couldn't die from strangulation and that it would put Percival in more trouble than he was ready to deal with.

"I don't know, maybe don't try it while I or one of the others are leaving," Constantine continued. "What did you think I'd do when I realized I couldn't close the door? Leave it open because I trust you?"

Percival wasn't going to answer because he didn't know what to say. Instead, he decided that distracting Constantine wouldn't be a bad thing. "Why are you doing this?" he asked.

"Doing what?"

"Going against the conclave. You're a hero. You should be protecting humanity."

"I should, and I am."

"You're actively working against the conclave. You're saving supernatural creatures."

"You know, I remember the history lessons the conclave gave us when we first became heroes. Have you ever wondered if they were telling us the truth?"

Percival blinked. "Why would they have lied?"

"Because it gives them what they want. The conclave isn't made up of good people, Percival. I know that nothing I can say will convince you of that, but the only things the conclave wants are power and to be rich. They'll do anything they can to obtain that, and that includes killing supernatural creatures who never hurt a human. They want control, and they can't control creatures, so they kill them."

Percival ignored most of what Constantine said. "Even if those creatures never attacked anyone, it doesn't mean they won't."

"Doesn't the same go for heroes? Or even humans, for that matter? Just like in every species, there are good people and bad ones. The bad ones are who the conclave should focus on, not supernatural beings who just want to be left in peace and live their life."

"Most supernatural beings are monsters."

Constantine looked disappointed, and Percival didn't understand why that made him feel bad. "If that's how you think still, then maybe we won't be able to convince you," Constantine murmured before stepping away and closing the door.

Percival didn't try to push it open. Instead, he listened to the beep of Constantine locking the door again and walking away.

The conclave did its best to protect humans. That was what the conclave and heroes were created for, and Percival clung to that. It had always been the conclave's job and honor to protect humanity. They didn't want power or anything else Constantine mentioned. They just wanted to keep everyone safe, or at least, everyone who deserved it.

But even though Percival was convinced of that and didn't want to think badly of the conclave, he couldn't help but think back over some of the missions he'd been on. Did the conclave really have to kill children to keep humanity safe? Sure, those children would one day become adults, and since they were supernatural creatures, they'd have the capacity to kill humans. They'd give the conclave trouble, so maybe it was better for the conclave to get rid of them before they could.

Yes. Percival had to remember how merciless those creatures were. They killed humans and heroes without a pause, and Percival's mission was to make sure they couldn't. As soon as he was out of this cell, he'd go back to it, and he'd tell the conclave everything he'd learned about the fallen heroes. The conclave would take care of them and make sure the fallen heroes couldn't hurt heroes or humans ever again.

And it would be thanks to Percival.

Chapter Two

Bayard regretted the promise he'd made to take care of Percival. It had taken work off Mordred, but at the same time, they still had to go over the emails and answer the ones that needed answering. Then they had to plan meetings with the heroes who wanted to know more about what the conclave was doing, make sure those meetings were safe, and attend them and try to convince the heroes that the conclave was using them.

He'd never been so busy. Taking care of things with the conclave didn't mean he and the others weren't still protecting supernatural creatures from them, which meant everyone had twice the work they had before. Hopefully, some of the heroes they'd been talking to would cross over and become part of their group, but it would be a while before they could trust them, and in the meantime, they had to do all the work.

And now, Bayard also had to talk to Percival and convince him the conclave was manipulating him and the other heroes.

He rubbed his forehead. He wanted to get out of this, and he knew that if he told Mordred it was too much, Mordred would let him go. The problem was that Mordred would take it on himself again, and that wasn't something Bayard could allow. Not only was Mordred working more than all of them, but he also had a personal life to deal with, and while Amyas was easy-going, he wouldn't allow Mordred to overwork himself. It was a good thing, but it was also a complication in this situation.

Bayard strode down the hallway, headed toward the

basement. That was where the cells were located, and where Percival had been staying since Bayard had dragged his unconscious ass to the house. Percival had never seen any other part of the place, which was how Bayard and Mordred had wanted things.

Not that Percival would be allowed to tell the conclave anything he might see here. If Mordred and Bayard couldn't convince him to cross over, they'd have to kill him. It was never an easy decision, but it had to be made, and Bayard and Mordred were used to it.

Their main goal was to protect the fallen heroes who had become their family. The goal after that was to protect supernatural creatures from the conclave, and after everything, if they could, to get rid of the conclave entirely. Bayard wasn't sure how that would work, because new heroes would always be born, and someone needed to take care of them, but he didn't think there was anything salvageable in the conclave. They were rotten to the core, and no amount of trying to fix it would work. Its foundations were gone, which meant they'd have to build new ones.

That was all in the future. Before they could do that, they had to take care of the conclave as it was today. And to do *that*, they needed manpower, hence Bayard's presence in the basement.

He opened the door, closed it again behind himself, and walked down the stairs. He could hear the TV on, and sure enough, when he got to the room where the guards spent their time, the screen was on. Bowen and Sybil, two of the four guards assigned to Percival, looked up. Sybil turned the TV off as they both got to their feet.

Bayard waved at them. "Stay. I don't need you to get up for me."

"You're here to visit Percival?" Bowen asked.

"I am. With everything going on, Mordred is too busy to

do this, so I volunteered. How's Percival?"

Sybil shrugged. "Not the nicest person I've ever talked to."

Bowen snorted. "That's an understatement. He keeps trying to escape. He's not friendly at all, no matter how many times you try talking to him. The only one still trying is Constantine, to be honest."

Bayard hadn't expected anything different, but he wished the situation was easier. As it was, it sounded like Percival was still in full hero mode, which meant he trusted the conclave entirely and probably wouldn't listen to him. That wouldn't stop Bayard from trying, but he had other things to do, dammit.

Bayard nodded. "What about now? What's he doing?"

"He reads a lot," Sybil said. "It might be worth sneaking some of those history books onto the shelves."

Bayard knew what books she was talking about. It was one of the things they used to make heroes see what the conclave was doing and had been doing for a long time. Those books had been written both by heroes who had defected and by supernatural creatures, which meant they had a point of view that wasn't the conclave's.

In the beginning, the conclave had been a good thing. Heroes were part of a small group of people who could kill supernatural creatures. They were born human and identified by a birthmark. Bayard had no idea how anyone had realized what the birthmark meant, but eventually, heroes had started fighting supernatural creatures and keeping humans safe. They'd slowly banded in groups, and those groups had become more numerous over time.

That was when the conclave was created. It was made up of older heroes who'd gone through hundreds of years of fighting and training. They located the humans with a birthmark, brought them into their fold, and trained them to kill supernatural creatures. And back then, it had been needed. It still was, in some cases, but these days, most creatures just wanted to be left in peace. The conclave should have allowed them that, maybe keeping an eye on them, but instead, they'd decided to kill all of them. Bayard still wasn't sure what they were trying to do, which was something they had to find out, but he wanted to focus on Percival for now.

"He's a little bitch," Bowen said.

Bayard arched a brow at him. "What do you mean?"

"No matter how many times we've tried to explain why we're here and why we left the conclave, he just doesn't believe anything we say. You can't argue with people like that. He'll only believe what he wants to believe, and it's not us. As far as I'm concerned, he's a lost cause."

"Isn't that how we all were in the beginning?"

"Maybe, but he's been here a while, and all of us have tried talking to him. He's a stubborn fuck. I wouldn't waste any more of my time on him, but you're the boss."

Bayard was dreading having to talk to Percival, but he'd volunteered, and he'd do it. Besides, they couldn't keep an enemy in their home for much longer. They had to decide whether Percival was worth keeping alive or if they should get rid of him. Bayard hoped for the first option, but it wasn't always possible, and it was something they had to face.

He sighed. "I see. Well, I'm headed to see him right now."

"Maybe you should bring him his lunch. That way, we won't have to do it," Bowen said.

"Trying to get out of your job?"

Bowen grinned. "I told you. The less I see him, the better I feel."

Bayard didn't berate Bowen for any of that. It was never easy to be on guard duty in this situation, but it was especially hard when the hero didn't want to listen to anything they had to say. That was what Percival was doing, and he was antagonizing his guards, except maybe Constantine, from what

Bowen had said.

Bayard made a mental note to talk to Constantine when he had the time. If he was still trying to get through to Percival, it meant he could see something in the hero that gave him hope. Bayard was going to need that.

Percival expected lunch, so he wasn't surprised when the door opened. What did surprise him was the man carrying the tray. Ever since he'd woken up here, he'd only seen the same four guards. This guy was none of those people, which made Percival sit up straighter. What was going on? Had the fallen heroes finally reached the limit of their patience? Were they going to kill him?

That was what he'd do in their place. They couldn't afford for a hero to go back to the conclave and tell them about what he'd seen while being a prisoner. That meant that either they managed to convince Percival to leave the conclave and work with them, or they killed him.

And they hadn't convinced Percival to do anything yet.

"Good morning," the man said.

Percival watched him without answering. Maybe it didn't have to be a bad thing. This was a new guy, which could mean Percival was about to be killed, but also that Percival might be able to manipulate him. He'd tried with the four guards, but it hadn't worked. Maybe it would this time.

He forced himself to smile. "Good morning."

If the man was surprised, he didn't show it. He put the tray down on the table after closing the door with his elbow, then looked around. "I see you've made yourself at home."

"There's not much else to do." Percival rose from the bed and took a tentative step forward. "I don't know you."

"My name is Bayard."

Constantine had mentioned Bayard. He was Mordred's

second, or at least, one of them. That didn't bode well for trying to manipulate him, but it wouldn't stop Percival. He *had* to try, if it was the last thing he did. "I'm Percival, but you already know that."

Bayard nodded. "I do. You should eat lunch before it gets cold."

Percival went to sit at the table. He picked up his fork and stabbed a piece of pasta with it, but he never glanced away from Bayard, even though the man looked like he'd barely noticed him. He was still poking around the cell, something that made Percival bristle. It might be a prison cell, but as it was, it was his home, and he didn't appreciate people touching his things.

Eventually, Bayard came to sit on the other side of the table. "I've heard you've been giving your guards trouble."

Percival shrugged. "I didn't attack them, if that's what you're asking."

"But you did try to run away."

"Wouldn't you have? I'm a prisoner. I don't want to be here."

"I would have, too. But maybe it would be a better idea for you to listen to what we have to say. I know you haven't been."

Percival had to resist the urge to snap at the guy. He took a deep breath, then forced himself to smile. "What your guards had to say wasn't interesting."

"Would you listen if I were the one telling you about it?"

The answer was no, but Percival shrugged again. "Maybe. You want me to leave the conclave behind. How am I supposed to do that? They're the only thing I've known for hundreds of years. They're my family."

"You mean they took you *away* from your family. That's what they do, isn't it?"

Percival couldn't deny that, but it was a necessary evil.

When children and teenagers were identified as heroes, they had to go through intensive training, and of course, the hero gene had to be triggered. That meant they had to die, and all of those things were best done in a controlled space. That way, they avoided things going badly. Bayard had to know that, yet he was ignoring it. Percival decided to go along with it. "I suppose it is," he murmured.

Bayard nodded. "Do you want to tell me about your family?"

Percival had no intention of talking about his family. "I'd like to ask for a favor."

Bayard's eyebrows rose, and he leaned back in his chair, crossing his arms over his chest. "A favor? I'm listening."

Percival didn't truly expect this to work, but he had to try. "I've been here a long time. I'd like to go outside."

Bayard didn't look surprised. "Outside, how?"

"Please. I promise I won't try to run away."

Bayard stared at Percival for so long it made Percival uncomfortable, and it convinced him Bayard had seen right through him. It wasn't a surprise, but he wished that wasn't the case. He just wanted to go home, dammit.

"You're trying to manipulate me, aren't you?" Bayard eventually asked.

"Why would I do that?"

Bayard snorted. "Because you're a prisoner. You were the one who told me I'd try to break out if I were in your place, and you're right. I would. I'd even sweet talk my captors if I had to, which is what you've been doing."

It was, and since he'd failed, Percival decided the best thing he could do was to keep his mouth shut from now on.

"You know, if I hadn't talked to the guards, it might have worked. But I know how you are with them. You tried to escape more times than I can count, and you're usually grumpy as shit. Yet with me, you're being sweet. What did you think

I'd do? Fall for your charms and take you outside so you could escape?"

Percival shook his head and looked away. He put his fork down, not hungry anymore, and stared at the wall.

"You should finish lunch," Bayard said when he realized Percival wouldn't answer.

When Percival didn't move to pick up his fork again, Bayard shrugged and picked it up himself. He pulled the plate closer and started eating, shocking Percival, who finally looked at him.

"That's my lunch," he said before he could stop himself.

"It was until you decided you weren't hungry anymore. Now it's mine, which is a good thing, since I have work to do once I leave this room."

He was trying to get a rise out of Percival, and unfortunately, it was working. Percival tried hard to keep a handle on his temper. He couldn't show Bayard he was getting to him.

Once he felt calmer, he turned his attention back to the wall.

"You know, I think all heroes are stubborn," Bayard said. "It's in our genetic makeup. We have to be, to do what we were created to do, don't we? But the conclave isn't something you should be stubborn about. I understand loyalty, but not when it's blind. Maybe you should start thinking about that instead of insisting you're a conclave hero. You'd realize the kind of monsters they are, and when you do, you'll understand what we're doing here."

Percival continued not answering.

Bayard sighed. "Come on. We don't have to be friends, but would it kill you to be friendly? Tell me anything. You haven't mentioned your family, even though I asked. What about them?"

"Why don't you tell me about yours?" Percival snapped.

He didn't expect Bayard to answer, mainly because family was usually a sore spot for heroes. Just like Bayard had said, they were taken away from their families as soon as the mark on their bodies was identified. They were never allowed to see their parents and siblings again, and it hurt. It still did, even though it had been hundreds of years since Percival had seen his father.

But Bayard nodded. "Sure. I was taken from them at seventeen. Let me tell you, it wasn't something I appreciated. I was lucky, because I was older than most heroes, and I managed to find them again a few years later."

Percival blinked. He wanted to ask many questions, and the first was how Bayard had done it. He was the first hero Percival knew about who'd found his family after being taken away from them. If the conclave had known about it, they'd have killed Bayard's family to make sure he couldn't sneak back to them. Heroes shouldn't have bonds. The only people they should care about were the conclave, and that hadn't changed over the centuries.

Was his family the reason Bayard had left the conclave? Wouldn't he be with them now if that was the case? Of course, his parents had no doubt died a long time ago, but how long had Bayard been on the run from the conclave?

Those were all questions Percival was dying to get an answer to but couldn't ask.

Bayard wasn't sure that telling Percival about his family was the best idea, but they'd been dead for a long time. He wouldn't mention that he kept in touch with their descendants, just in case Percival managed to escape and run back to the conclave. His family was the one thing Bayard wasn't willing to risk, be it his human one or the fallen heroes.

Still, he wanted Percival to remember his family. He

wanted him to see how cruel it was to take children away from their parents and never allow them back.

He cleared his throat. Percival wasn't talking, but he *was* listening, and it was better than nothing.

"Like I said, I was seventeen when a hero traveled to my village. Unfortunately for me, the mark is on my arm, so he was able to see it easily. He took me away that same night. I was angry, and I didn't understand what was happening. I just wanted to go back to my parents and my siblings. Instead, I was taken to the conclave."

Bayard paused. Those were some of the hardest memories he had. Besides, Percival no doubt remembered how it was. He'd been through it, too.

"I can't remember how many times the heroes beat me," he continued. "I didn't want to train. I didn't care about super-natural creatures or anything like that. I just wanted to go home."

Bayard had seen many other children and teenagers go through the same thing. The conclave tried not to waste — as they thought of it — any hero they got their hands on, but sometimes, they had to get rid of those they couldn't train or manipulate. Bayard had seen many of the teenagers he lived with disappear and never come back.

"But eventually, I realized I was going at it the wrong way. If I wanted to see my parents again, it wouldn't do me any good to be beaten up and possibly killed. So I gave in. I started doing what the trainers ordered, and eventually I became a full-fledged hero. It took a few years for the conclave and my superiors to trust me and send me on missions on my own. As soon as they did, I went looking for my family. They were where I'd left them, in our village."

Bayard could remember the moment he'd walked through the door of his childhood home. He hadn't knocked, because he'd never had to. His mother had been in the kitchen, peeling carrots, and she'd dropped everything when she'd seen him. He'd never forget her cry, the rush of her feet on the floor, her arms around him.

He'd known even then that if he wasn't careful and if he didn't go back to the conclave, they'd kill his parents and siblings and everyone he held dear. That was why he'd sat his parents down and explained what had happened. They'd had a hard time believing it, but in the end, they wanted him to be safe, and the only way to make that happen was to allow him to go back.

So they had.

"I'm not saying you went through the same thing," he continued. "But I know enough heroes and their stories to think that you probably did. The conclave was never nice about taking children away from their parents. They never tried talking to the parents and explaining what was happening."

Percival snorted. "Because you think your parents would have handed you over to the conclave if they had?"

Bayard resisted the urge to grin because he'd made Percival talk. "Probably not. But maybe being a hero shouldn't be something that is forced on you. We have no say in how we are born, but we should have a say in what we want to do with our lives. Not everyone is made to be a hero, no matter what the mark on our bodies says."

"We were chosen before we were even born," Percival said, finally looking at Bayard again. "It's an honor. Of course we're made to be heroes. We wouldn't be chosen otherwise."

Bayard hadn't eaten much of Percival's pasta, and he put the fork down, pushing the plate toward Percival again. Percival was so intent on watching Bayard that he didn't even pause before picking the fork up again.

"Maybe, maybe not," Bayard said. "But I'm sure you saw what happened to the children who either refused to do this or were incapable of doing it. How many of those kids disappeared? How many never came back?"

Bayard knew the answer. It was all of them, because the conclave didn't give second chances. If the children they kidnapped didn't become heroes, they were taken care of. The conclave couldn't waste time and resources on children who wouldn't give them back anything. They also didn't give them back to their parents, because someone was bound to ask questions.

Bayard leaned closer to the table. "If anything, ask yourself this. Does the conclave have to kill children because they don't do what the conclave wants? Wouldn't it be better to ask those kids what they wanted to do before taking them, or give them back to their parents?"

He watched Percival as he picked at his food. He hoped he'd gotten through, but somehow, he didn't think this was how Mordred usually did things. There was no way Mordred would tell anyone about his family. Bayard probably shouldn't have, either, especially considering he was still in contact with them. It had felt right, though, and he didn't regret it—much.

Percival shook his head. "The conclave does what they have to do. Where would we be if the children chosen to be heroes didn't train? Supernatural creatures would overrun the world. Yes, it's a pity so many children are taken away from their parents, but it has to be done. It's a sacrifice all heroes have to go through, and it's one of the things that makes us stronger."

Bayard sighed and leaned back in his chair. He hadn't expected this to be easy or for Percival to be convinced after one conversation, but he'd hoped to crack Percival's conviction that the conclave could do no wrong. He didn't seem to have, and he suspected that insisting wouldn't change anything. Percival was clinging to what he knew and the belief that the conclave was good, and he wouldn't accept anything else.

Hopefully, that would change, and soon.

Bayard got to his feet to leave. Percival's eyes widened, and he reached for Bayard, stopping before actually touching him. "What are you doing?" Percival asked.

"Leaving. I have work to do, and it's obvious you won't listen to reason."

"It's because I've been here for a long time. I need to do something, to see something different. Please. I'm sure that if you take me outside, we could talk there, and it would be easier for me to wrap my mind around all of this."

Bayard had to give it to Percival — he wasn't giving up, and he wasn't afraid of trying something that sounded ridiculous, like begging Bayard to let him out. "We can talk about this again soon."

Percival scowled. "You're not going to convince me of anything by keeping me a prisoner."

"Maybe not. I can't allow you to leave the cell, though, and you know it."

Bayard picked up the tray and moved toward the door. He didn't look back as he unlocked it and stepped out. He didn't think he'd made any progress, but he still had hope. He couldn't lose it, not when the only other option would be to kill Percival. Maybe they would have to eventually, but Bayard wasn't done trying.

Too many heroes had died already, children and adults who'd worked for the conclave for decades. Even though they were enemies, they were also Bayard's brothers and sisters, and he didn't want to have to kill any of them. He would if he had to, but for now, there was still a chance Percival would listen to reason, and Bayard wouldn't waste it.

CHAPTER THREE

Percival wasn't feeling well, and he knew what his problem was. That was why he'd tried to escape so many times. It was why he needed to go back to the conclave, and why he might die if he didn't.

He swallowed and stared at the ceiling. He needed the pills, but there was no way for him to get them. He couldn't explain to the fallen heroes what the pills he needed were for. And they *would* ask. Heroes didn't get sick, so they didn't need medication. Besides, they might recognize what the pills were for, and once they did, everything would be lost for Percival. The fallen heroes would know what he was, and they'd use it against him. They might even contact the conclave to let them know, which meant Percival wouldn't have a home to go back to.

He swallowed. He couldn't tell the fallen heroes about his pills, but how else was he supposed to get them? The answer was that he couldn't, which freaked him out. He hadn't been without those meds since before he'd become a full-fledged hero, and he didn't know what to do.

He sat up. Usually he could ignore what he was. He'd been doing it for hundreds of years, and with the pills, it was easy. It wouldn't be once his siren half took over, though. There would be no way for him to ignore it, which was why he forced himself to think about it now.

He licked his lips. He hadn't allowed his siren side out in hundreds of years, not since before he'd been taken. As soon as his father had realized what Percival could do, he'd made sure Percival could block that ability. It was the only thing that had allowed him to survive as he trained to become a hero, then later, as he became one. If the conclave had ever found out about it, they wouldn't have hesitated to kill Percival.

Percival didn't doubt that the fallen heroes would let the conclave know as soon as they found out about it, which was why he couldn't allow it to happen. But what was he supposed to do? He couldn't go anywhere. He couldn't request more pills. He'd soon become dangerous, and he didn't know how to deal with it. He hadn't had to deal with his siren half since he was a child. He didn't know how powerful it was or how to keep it under control.

Most days, he wished he could reach inside himself and tear the siren half out. What good had it ever done him? He'd never known his mother, and he'd never wanted to know her, especially not after he'd realized what she'd cursed him with.

So, he had to make sure the fallen heroes didn't find out what he was and what he could do. How would he do that?

The sound of footsteps made him tense. Was it already lunchtime? He didn't want any of the fallen heroes to find him in a vulnerable position, so he rose from the bed and went to sit at the table. Hopefully, it would be Bowen, who never stopped to chat the way Constantine did. Percival's siren felt like it was just under the surface of his skin, but if he could keep it at bay for a bit longer, he might be able to send it dormant again. He didn't know how well it would work without pills, but he'd try. That would be impossible if Constantine stopped to chat.

He stared at the door as it opened and almost groaned when he saw who was on the other side. He'd hoped it wasn't Constantine, but he would have preferred him to Bayard. The fallen hero was here to continue trying to convince Percival he should betray the conclave. That was a good thing, because as long as he thought he could do that, it would give Percival more time to try to find a way out of here, but Bayard was the last person Percival wanted to see right now.

Bayard grinned as he moved toward the table. "Hello. I brought you lunch."

Percival crossed his arms over his chest. "I can see that."

"And I see someone is grumpy today."

"I'm grumpy because I'm stuck here." Percival swallowed. "Please. I just want to go outside. You can tie me up if you want. I just need some fresh air and to feel the wind on my skin."

While Percival was saying this because he wanted Bayard to soften and take him outside, he couldn't deny to himself that it was the truth. He did want to feel the wind on his skin.

In the beginning, he'd tried counting the days that had passed since he'd been taken. It hadn't been easy, since he'd been unconscious when he'd arrived, but he didn't think that had lasted very long. He'd stopped counting after thirty days, and he didn't care anymore. The conclave wasn't coming for him, but then, they never came for anyone. If Percival was going to get away from the fallen heroes, he'd have to do it on his own, which was what he'd been trying to do since day one. Unfortunately for him, it hadn't worked—yet. It still might, even though the chances it would were getting lower every day.

Bayard put the tray on the table as he shook his head. "You know I can't do that."

Percival shot to his feet. "Why not?" he asked in a harsh voice. He was angry, and he wanted to punch something, preferably Bayard's face. "It's not like I can go anywhere, can I? You'll keep an eye on me, and you could tie me up. I could even promise I won't try anything."

"And I should believe that? How many times have you tried to escape?"

"You'd have done the exact same thing if you were in my place."

"I would have, and I would also be begging to be let out. You have to try anything to escape, don't you?"

Percival screamed. He needed an outlet for his anger. Trying to hurt Bayard wouldn't help. If anything, it would make the situation even worse, and if Percival was going to have one chance to escape, he couldn't afford that to happen. Instead of attacking Bayard like he wanted to, he turned around and hit the wall with his fist.

The stone and plaster crumbled under his knuckles. Pain pulsed in his hand, but it also felt so good. Percival panted. The room swirled around him to the point where he was almost afraid he'd faint.

"Are you done throwing your tantrum?" Bayard asked from behind Percival.

Percival sucked in a breath, then another. He lowered his hand, not one bit surprised to see blood on his fingers. He wiggled them, wincing at the discomfort. Maybe he shouldn't have hit the wall. As it was, an injury would make his escape even harder, which was another thing he couldn't afford. Unfortunately for him, he hadn't thought before acting, and now, he was stuck with a bloody hand and a temper problem.

Bayard wasn't surprised at the way Percival had reacted. He'd been pushing the man every time they saw each other. Percival was resisting, although that wasn't surprising, either.

It was the first time Percival became so angry. Bayard knew better than to try to intervene, so he let Percival punch the wall and made a mental note it would have to be fixed as soon as possible. The punch seemed to have been enough to get the anger out of Percival, and he shook his hand, staring at his bloody knuckles. Bayard waited for Percival to answer his question, but Percival didn't.

Bayard sighed. He hoped he was breaking through, but he couldn't be a hundred percent sure, and it worried him. He didn't want Percival to hurt himself, not if he was going to become a friend.

Bayard took a step forward. "You're bleeding."

"It's not the first time I've hurt myself."

Bayard arched a brow. "Should I be worried?"

Percival snorted. "I'm not suicidal, if that's what you're asking."

Bayard hadn't been asking that, but he was relieved to get confirmation. Percival had been trying to manipulate him since the first day they'd talked, and Bayard wouldn't have put it past him to play that card, too.

He strode to the door and punched the code in. He wanted to get something to wrap Percival's hand. He was worried about Percival, which was the only excuse he could find for what happened next.

An arm wrapped around his neck. Percival squeezed, maybe to strangle him, maybe to incapacitate him. Whatever the reason, Bayard couldn't allow him to do that.

"Just let me go. I won't hurt you," Percival said.

Bayard went slack. It was enough for Percival to stumble back, but he didn't let go. Bayard stomped his foot onto Percival's, then elbowed him in his gut. Percival howled and let him go, and Bayard turned around, ready to hurt him if he had to.

He did. Percival was charging him, his gaze desperate. The cell door was open, and he wanted out. Luckily for Bayard, he was older and better trained, especially after Percival had been sitting in the cell for a while.

Percival punched Bayard on the cheek. It hurt, but it wasn't the first time that happened. Bayard took the punch. Then, even though he didn't want to hurt Percival, he hit him in the gut.

Percival folded in two. His cheeks were flushed, and his too-long hair was all over the place. He was holding his stomach, and Bayard figured he'd had enough. He didn't try to attack again, but Bayard stayed ready, just in case.

"They warned me you'd try to escape," he said.

Percival looked at the open door, but instead of moving toward it like Bayard expected, he flopped back onto one of the chairs at the table. "I'd have beaten you if I weren't so weak," he said.

"And why are you weak? You haven't been eating enough."

"I should have."

He was right, but Bayard was glad he hadn't. Not that he would have gone anywhere. Even if he'd managed to escape the cell, he would have found himself in a room with two guards. If he'd managed to beat them up, too, well, the house was full of fallen heroes who knew he was a prisoner and wouldn't hesitate to beat him up and drag him back to his cell. Besides, the house was alarmed, although that was to keep people out rather than in.

Percival buried his hands into his hair. He looked desperate, and while Bayard understood and wanted to help, he couldn't do much for now. The only thing that would make Percival happy was to be allowed to leave, and that wasn't something Bayard could give him.

Percival looked at Bayard. "Please. I just want to leave."

Bayard was surprised that he wanted to say yes. There was something in Percival's tone that pulled Bayard in. It made him want to say yes to anything Percival suggested, so much so that he even took a step toward Percival.

Percival's eyes widened, and he asked again, "*Please.* Let me go."

The pull was there again, demanding Bayard obey. It was

hard to resist, and Bayard was confused and angry. He didn't want to risk it, so instead, he stepped out into the hallway and closed the door again, locking it.

Percival got to his feet. "I just want to be let go. I promise I won't tell anyone where this place is," he said.

Bayard glared at him. "What are you doing?"

"Nothing. I'm just talking to you."

That seemed to be the truth, but there had to be more to it. Even though Bayard could admit he liked Percival, he didn't like him so much that he'd risk his family to let him go. It didn't matter how gorgeous Percival was or how much he looked like wounded puppy at the moment.

"I'm going to get something for your hand," Bayard stopped. The anger made it easier to think through Percival's words. "You better start eating. If you're planning on trying to escape again, you're going to need the energy."

"Why aren't you starving me?" Percival asked.

His voice was normal now, or at least, Bayard was reacting to it in a normal way. What the fuck had happened? "Is that what the conclave would do?" he asked.

"You know it is. You were a conclave hero for long enough."

Bayard nodded and took a step forward, closer to the cell door. "That's what I'm trying to make you see. We're not like the conclave. We don't starve our prisoners, even though it means they could try to escape. One day, you'll realize I'm right, and you'll give in."

That was the wrong thing to say, because Percival's expression hardened. "The conclave is my home and my family, and they protect humanity. You'll never convince me otherwise."

Bayard sighed. "You know what's going to happen if we don't," he murmured.

The knowledge was in Percival's gaze, but he didn't say anything. Instead, he continued watching Bayard as he walked down the hallway toward the guards' room. They'd have bandages and something for the pain if Percival wanted it.

This wasn't what Bayard had expected would happen when he'd decided to visit Percival this morning, and he had even more questions about the man than he had before. He wasn't sure he'd ever get any answers, but he was stubborn. Given enough time, he *knew* he could break down Percival's protective shell, and hopefully convince him to see the conclave the way it really was.

In the meantime, he would focus on fixing Percival's hand, because it was one thing he knew for sure how to do.

Percival's ability had leaked through. He hadn't meant for that to happen, and he'd never actively used it that he could remember, which was probably why it hadn't worked. He'd seen it, though. When he'd asked Bayard to let him go, Bayard had wanted to.

That was what being a siren was. Percival could convince people to do what he wanted using his voice. The pills he usually took blocked that ability so that Percival was as normal as any other hero. He hadn't been taking them for a month, though, and the effects were vanishing.

He was surprised it hadn't happened sooner. He'd expected it to, and maybe it had. He wouldn't know, since he hadn't used the ability since he was a child, when his father had realized what was going on and had made sure Percival knew how dangerous it was. He'd thought the people in their village would hurt Percival if they found out what he could do, and the herbs had become even more important once the conclave had found Percival and had taken him away.

And now, Percival was without them for the first time in hundreds of years, and his ability was showing. How was he supposed to control it? Better yet, could he use it to convince Bayard or one of the guards to let him out? It had almost worked, but not quite, which meant the ability was still hiding under a layer of medicine. That wouldn't last long, and while the thought terrified Percival and made him feel like a freak and a monster, if using his ability was what it took to be free, he would.

The problem was that he didn't know how to do it. Was he just supposed to talk and want the person he was talking with to do what he wanted? Or was there more to it?

It didn't look like it. He'd asked Bayard to be let out, and Bayard had almost done it. Maybe next time Percival tried, he'd manage.

The door opened again. Percival was still in his chair, and he didn't look up. He already knew it was Bayard. He'd said he would get something for Percival's hand, and while Percival didn't actually need anything, he was grateful for the moment of respite. It was over, so he straightened in his chair and watched as Bayard walked into the cell and closed it behind himself, locking it again.

They stared at each other for a moment. The reason Percival had retreated and stopped trying to influence Bayard was that he was afraid of what he could do, yes, but also because he didn't want Bayard to realize what he was. What would happen if he did?

It was easy to know what the conclave would do if they ever found out that Percival was half siren. Supernatural creatures were monsters, as were their offspring. Percival would be killed without remorse and without thinking twice about it.

The fallen heroes were different. They protected supernatural creatures, but that wasn't what Percival was, was it? He might be half siren, but he was all hero, and he worked for the conclave. The fallen heroes probably wouldn't hesitate to kill him.

"Will you attack me again?" Bayard asked.

Percival shook his head. He was too weak to win, and now that he knew his ability was awakening, he couldn't afford to fail a second time. If he was going to do this, if he was going to use his ability to escape, he needed food and rest and not to tire himself out doing something that would fail.

Bayard put everything he was holding on the table and reached for Percival's hand. Percival didn't react, even though he wanted to pull away, especially when Bayard started poking at the knuckles. It hurt, but Percival kept his gaze on the wall in front of him.

"You knew you wouldn't get anywhere," Bayard murmured.

Percival heard the crinkle of plastic. Then something damp touched his knuckles. He hissed at the burn but still didn't look at Bayard.

Bayard sighed. "You're angry. I get it, and you're right. I'd try escaping, too, if I were in your place. There's only one way you'll leave this cell alive, though, and you need to accept that. You have to listen to what I and the others have to say. We're not lying to you. We've been working for the conclave and watching them for hundreds of years, longer than you've been alive. We know everything there is to know about the conclave, and that includes their secrets. If only you opened your mind and allowed me to show you what the conclave has been doing, you wouldn't be so loyal to them."

Percival couldn't allow Bayard to make him change his mind. The conclave was created to protect humanity, and Percival was one of its warriors. It was an honor, and he'd never do anything that could hurt the conclave or that could make him lose that job. What he was didn't matter. He'd managed to ignore and snuff out his siren half for hundreds of years. He would do it again as soon as he was free of the cell.

He had to, because if he didn't, the conclave wouldn't hesitate to kill him.

Thankfully, Bayard stopped talking and trying to convince Percival. He worked in silence, cleaning the wounds on Percival's knuckles, then wrapping them as well as he could. By the time he was finished, Percival's hand ached, but he welcomed the pain.

It made it easier not to listen to Bayard's words.

"Eat your lunch. I can't promise I'll be back tomorrow, but I'll try," Bayard said as he moved toward the door. He kept an eye on Percival, but Percival stayed where he was. He wasn't going to attack Bayard again. He knew he'd lose this time, too, and he wasn't ready to face that.

He had to be smart about this. If he wanted to be free, if he wanted to make sure Bayard and the other fallen heroes didn't find out what he was, he had to be more careful and stop being an idiot.

He had to think about this carefully and find a way out of the cell. That was the only thing that mattered and the one thing he had to keep in mind.

Chapter Four

Bayard was still thinking about what had happened with Percival the next day. He needed to know more about the hero, and there was only one way to obtain that, since Percival wouldn't talk to him.

He knocked on the door of Mordred's office.

Once, he wouldn't have hesitated to open the door as soon as he was done knocking. The last time he'd done that, though, he'd walked in on Mordred and Amyas having fun on Mordred's desk, and that was an image he'd never be able to forget. Now, he knocked, and every time he was in the office, he couldn't help but stare at the desk.

"Come in," Mordred called out.

Bayard pushed open the door and screwed his eyes shut. "Is there anything I shouldn't see?"

"Very funny. And do I have to remind you that the only reason you saw something you shouldn't have was that you didn't wait for me to tell you to enter?"

Bayard grinned and closed the door behind himself. Mordred was alone, although Amyas probably wasn't far. He never was these days, but Bayard didn't mind. Amyas made Mordred happy, and that was all Bayard wanted.

"To what do I owe this pleasure?" Mordred asked.

Bayard sat on the other side of Mordred's desk. "I have a few questions about Percival."

Mordred looked surprised. "Why? Do you think that knowing more about him will help you convince him?"

"Well, possibly, but that's not the reason." Bayard

hesitated.

He didn't know what had happened, and he was probably wrong. There was no way Percival could do anything a normal hero couldn't do. Still, he couldn't forget the way he'd wanted to do anything Percival asked or that he'd been about to free him. There was something there, and Bayard had to find out what it was because it could be dangerous. He'd been able to resist this time, but he might not the next, and what about the guards? From what he knew, Constantine spent a lot of time with Percival. What if Percival tried to manipulate him the way he had Bayard yesterday?

"You're worrying me. Has something happened?" Mordred asked.

"Tell me what you know about him first." Bayard didn't want Mordred to be influenced by what he told him, just in case.

Mordred's eyebrows were high on his forehead, but he nodded. "Well, there's not much I can tell you. I don't know him, although I've tried looking into him. He's been a hero for close to three hundred years. He was born in Britain, and while I couldn't find anything on his mother, his father was a normal enough person. He looked for his son for years after Percival was taken."

That was nothing new. Many heroes had parents who were still looking for them even as they reached the end of their lives. Of course, many heroes also had parents who didn't care, but that wasn't the case here.

Bayard was curious about Percival's mother. It seemed hard to believe that there was nothing to find about her, especially considering how careful the conclave was when selecting heroes. They took in everyone who had the mark, but not all of those people became full-fledged heroes. A lot disappeared, whether because of how they behaved or, like Bayard suspected, because there was something odd in their family.

Was that what had happened here? If Percival's mother had been a supernatural creature, surely the conclave would know about it. But even Mordred hadn't been able to find out anything about her. Maybe the same had been true for the conclave.

"As far as his work as a hero, it's pretty normal," Mordred continued. "He obeys orders. He does what the conclave asks when they ask it, and he's proud of it. I talked to a few of our fallen heroes, and they all agreed on that. Percival doesn't have friends or anyone he's close to, but that could be as much because of the conclave and their rules as because of him."

Mordred crossed his arms over his chest. Bayard knew he wanted to ask, but he was giving him time to get his thoughts into order. Bayard was grateful, because he still had no idea what to think about any of this.

He cleared his throat. "I went to talk to Percival yesterday. He's getting impatient, and he wants to be let out. He even punched the wall because he got angry at me."

Mordred winced. "We'll have to fix that. Is he okay?"

"His knuckles will be bruised, but he's fine. That's not what worries me. When he asked me to be let out, I wanted to do it."

Mordred sighed. "I know this isn't an easy job, but —"

"You don't understand. I know I can't let him go. I don't want to let him go because he'd go straight back to the conclave. But there was a compulsion in me to do what he wanted. I almost did, too. I managed to stop myself, but it's obvious something was wrong, and we need to know what it was."

Mordred leaned forward, even more interested now. "What did it feel like?"

Bayard was relieved Mordred didn't doubt him. He doubted himself, and the more he thought about it, the less possible this sounded to him. Still, he couldn't dismiss it.

He thought back to how it had felt when Percival had tried to get him to free him. "Well, he begged to be let go, saying he just wanted some fresh air. I don't know what it was in his voice or whatever he was doing, but I wanted to give him that. I wanted that just because he did. I wanted to do what he wanted me to do."

Mordred frowned. "That sounds like a kind of compulsion."

"It does, which is why I'm worried. I managed to resist, but what if I can't next time? What if one of the guards can't?"

Mordred swore. "This is the last thing we needed."

Bayard was sorry to bring up even more problems, but Mordred had to know. Besides, it wasn't impossible to solve. "We already have two different codes for the doors that lead to the cell. We have to make sure the guards only know one of them. That way, even if they open the door to Percival's cell, he won't be going anywhere."

"That's a good idea, but we have to do something about Percival. Do you know where he could have gotten that kind of ability?"

"What ability?" Amyas asked as he strode in through the door that led to the garden.

His cheeks were flushed, and he'd clearly been in the sun. He'd stuck a flower behind his ear, and his blond hair created a halo around his face. He looked like an angel.

Bayard looked away when Amyas reached Mordred. He wanted to give them some privacy, but he couldn't leave, not when discussing something this important.

"So?" Amyas asked as he leaned back after kissing Mordred. "What ability? And who has it?"

"Percival," Mordred explained. He waved at Bayard to continue.

"He asked me to let him go yesterday, and I wanted to do it, as in, I felt like I should obey him. It was almost like a compulsion."

Amyas's eyes widened. "That sounds like a siren."

Bayard shook his head. "That's not possible. Percival is a hero. He can't be a siren."

Amyas shrugged. "Maybe not a siren. I'm sure other creatures can do that. He does sound like one, though. They can compel people to do things just by asking. It's their ability."

It did sound like Percival, but how was it possible?

"Well, we don't know anything about Percival's mother," Mordred said.

"But the conclave would have known if she was a siren. They would have killed Percival."

"I could talk to him," Amyas offered.

Bayard wasn't going to touch that with a ten-foot pole. If Amyas wanted to talk to Percival, he needed to ask Mordred.

"Why do you want to talk to him?" Mordred asked.

"Because if he *is* a siren, he won't be able to influence me. Both sirens and undines are water creatures. We often live together, which is, I think, one of the reasons we can resist the compulsion. Even if he tries, he won't be able to get me to do anything I don't want to do. I think it's the only way for you to know what he is as quickly as possible."

Mordred didn't look convinced, but he nodded anyway. Bayard knew he'd been making an effort to let Amyas make his own decisions and try not to be overprotective, and this sounded like it was part of that.

Amyas beamed. "I'll bring him food." He kissed Mordred on the cheek. "And don't worry about me. I'll be fine."

Bayard hoped he would, be because if he wasn't, Mordred would reign hell on Percival — and on anyone else who hadn't protected Amyas, including him.

Percival gritted his teeth and pushed back at the siren half. It wanted out now that it had a taste of freedom, but Percival couldn't allow that. There was no way to know if he'd be able to suppress it again, even with the pills, and he wasn't willing to risk it. Besides, there also was no way to know how it would change him.

He'd never known his mother, so he had no idea what she'd looked like. His father had tried to explain, but he'd still been in love with her, and he'd had nothing but good things to say. Apparently, she had long blonde hair and blue eyes, and she was beautiful. That was all Percival knew, and it wasn't helpful. What if he allowed his siren half to peek through and ended up with gills or something like that?

He was relieved when he heard footsteps coming closer. He didn't want to talk to anyone, least of all Bayard or Constantine, but they'd be a welcome distraction. Maybe if he focused on something else for a bit, it would be easier for him to ignore the siren wanting out.

Percival stayed in this chair as he listened to whoever was there unlock the door. It opened, and Percival was surprised to see not one of the guards or Bayard but Amyas, the undine. He hadn't seen him since the lake, and he had no idea what Amyas might want from him.

He tensed, staring at the undine. Amyas was carrying a tray, and he walked toward the table where Percival was sitting after closing the door. He put the tray onto the table, then sat on the empty chair and stared.

Percival might not want to talk to him, but after a few seconds of staring, he couldn't stand it anymore.

"What do you want?" he snapped.

Amyas grinned. "Nothing. I brought you some food. I thought you'd enjoy it."

Percival looked at the tray. He'd already eaten lunch, but this wasn't a meal. It looked more like a snack, and it had been a while since he'd eaten cake.

"Why did you bring me cake?"

Amyas shrugged. "I like cake. A lot of people like cake, and I thought you might, too. I can eat it if you don't want it."

Percival reached for the tray and pulled it closer. "Where's Bayard?"

"He's busy. Why? Would you have preferred him to come?"

"Of course not. What I would prefer is to be let go."

Amyas wasn't a fighter like the guards or Bayard. If Percival managed to overpower him, he might be able to escape.

But maybe he wouldn't have to overpower him. His siren ability had been waking up more and more as the time passed, and even though he hadn't convinced Bayard to do what he wanted, that was yesterday. Maybe now he had enough power to do it. Besides, Bayard had almost obeyed.

Percival ate a forkful of cake as he pondered what to do next. The easiest and safest thing to do was probably to convince Amyas to let him out. If he had Amyas with him, the fallen heroes wouldn't attack. He could compel Amyas to stay with him until he was out of this place.

Percival focused on Amyas. "I'm glad to see you," he said, unsure how to do this.

Amyas blinked. "You are?"

Percival nodded. "But you know what would make me even happier? I want to get out of here. I want to breathe some fresh air. Do you think you can help me with that?"

"What do you want me to do?" Amyas asked.

Percival was almost there. He sucked in a breath, then said, "I'd like you to unlock the door. Once it's unlocked, you'll come with me. We can go outside."

"And when we're outside?"

Was Amyas supposed to be asking so many questions while Percival was compelling him? Percival had no idea, so he pushed on. "I'll keep you with me until I'm sure it's safe.

Then, I'll allow you to go back to your boyfriend. You have to make sure nothing happens to me, though. You'll have to stay close to me."

Amyas stared.

Percival wasn't sure what else to do. "Amyas? Do it now. Open the door for me." Percival put all of his ability into words. He had no idea how to do this, but that wouldn't stop him from trying.

Amyas got to his feet. Percival held his breath, waiting for Amyas to obey.

But instead, Amyas looked at Percival and put his hands on his hips. "Nice try, but it's not going to work on me."

Percival frowned. "What do you mean?" There was no way Amyas knew what Percival had been trying to do.

"The compulsion. You're part siren, aren't you?"

Percival shook his head. Panic gripped his chest, and he had to get Amyas to believe he was wrong. He couldn't admit what he was to anyone, least of all an enemy.

"I'm an undine," Amyas said.

"I know." Because Percival had been sent to fight Amyas's tribe, and he'd failed spectacularly.

"Like undines, sirens are water creatures. We often live in the same villages, and the sirens' compulsion ability doesn't work on us. That's why I was the one who came in today. Bayard said he felt something strange yesterday, and he was afraid that you'd compel whoever came into your cell next to let you out. And you did. You failed because your ability doesn't work on me."

Amyas continued staring. His gaze made Percival's skin itch. He needed Amyas to forget about everything he'd just realized. He couldn't afford for anyone to know what he was. What would Amyas do with that knowledge?

"You don't have to answer," Amyas continued. "I can't say I understand you or how you were able to become a hero

48

since you're part supernatural creature, but it's none of my business. I'm not going to look the other way, though. I know what you are and what you're trying to do. My loyalty is to Mordred and the fallen heroes, not to you or the sirens."

He turned around to leave. Percival wanted to stop him, yet at the same time, he didn't. He didn't want Amyas to continue staring at him, not now that he knew Percival's secret. He also didn't want Amyas to leave and tell whoever was waiting outside what happened.

He got to his feet when Amyas reached the door, but Amyas noticed him moving. He turned around, one hand on the door, the other hanging by his side. "You're not so stupid that you're going to attack me, are you?" he asked.

"I just want to be free," Percival croaked.

Amyas nodded. "I understand that. I wanted to be free from my tribe, and I am now. There's only one way you'll obtain that, and you know it." He unlocked the door, and before Percival could say anything else, he was out, and the door closed behind him.

Percival stared. What would Amyas do? There was no doubt in Percival's mind that Amyas was already telling Mordred what he'd found, and while Percival was already in the fallen heroes' hands, he knew things would become even worse now. He didn't know how bad they would turn or what the fallen heroes would do with him, but of one thing, he was sure.

He wouldn't like whatever was going to happen next.

Bayard was bouncing his knee. He and Mordred were in the guards' room with Constantine and Sybil, who were on shift right now. Constantine looked like he was about to explode as he tried not asking too many questions, and while Sybil was curious, she didn't seem to care as much as Constantine.

It was probably because she'd been a fallen hero for much longer, while Constantine had only been with them for a few decades. He could remember well how he'd become a fallen hero, which was no doubt why he felt so close to Percival.

The door to the hallway where the cells were located opened. Bayard tensed, even though he'd heard someone punch in the code. It could only be Amyas, and sure enough, he stepped into the room, closing the door behind himself. His gaze went straight to Mordred, who rushed to his side to make sure he was okay.

Amyas smiled and allowed him to do whatever he wanted. Bayard was impatient, but not impatient enough to deny them a few moments. Once he had, he cleared his throat. Those two would never stop being affectionate if someone didn't stop them. "What did you find out?" he asked.

"That I was right. He's half siren."

Bayard had expected that after the conversation they'd had in the office, but he was still surprised. "He told you that?"

Amyas shook his head. "He didn't have to. He tried to compel me to take him outside. He even said I had to stay with him until I was sure he was safe."

Mordred growled. "He would have used you as a hostage?"

"Which is exactly what you did to escape from my tribe," Amyas pointed out.

"Only because you were okay with me doing that."

"I was. But he couldn't compel me, so stop worrying about that. I felt his ability, and when I told him I knew what he was, he acted like nothing was wrong. He knows I know, though. I'm sure of that. I'm also sure he's freaking out because he doesn't know what you're going to do with this knowledge."

Bayard leaned back in his chair. What *could* they do with this knowledge? They could force Percival to stay away from the conclave. If they told the conclave what Percival was, they wouldn't hesitate to execute him. That was what made it so hard to understand why Percival was still loyal to them. He had to know what the conclave would do to him if they found out about this. It was a miracle they hadn't already, and Bayard was curious to know how they didn't know. But if they did, Percival *would* die, yet he still didn't believe the conclave was doing anything wrong. They thought he was a monster just because of how he was born and who his parents were. How could he not see how wrong that was?

"How is this possible?" Mordred asked. "The conclave would have killed him if they found out about this, so they can't know. But they investigate the families of the children they identify as heroes. They should have found out about this."

"Not unless Percival's mother was the siren," Bayard said. "You couldn't find anything on her, and while it might be because of how much time has passed, what if Percival's father knew what she was? What if he made sure no one ever knew about it because he wanted to protect her and their son?"

"That's certainly possible, but it still doesn't explain why Percival works for the conclave."

"Why did any of us work for the conclave? After a while, we felt we belonged there and that the conclave was our family. If that's what happened, then maybe Percival being half siren doesn't have anything to do with this. The conclave took him from his father, trained and raised him. That's why he's loyal to them."

"But he has to know they'd kill him if they knew."

Bayard shrugged. "He probably does. It doesn't mean he can't ignore it."

Even though it was dangerous. But if Percival had been hiding what he was for most of his life, it was ingrained in him. He had to think he'd be able to get out of this, whatever happened. And he might be right. Unless he used his ability during his missions for the conclave, there was probably no way for anyone to find out about it. The only reason Bayard had was that Percival had tried using his ability on him.

"Either way, this is a problem," Mordred said. "He could compel one of the guards to let him out."

"That's why we'll implement the change about the codes," Bayard said. He'd already explained to Sybil and Constantine what they should do. They'd changed the code of the door to the hallway, and only Constantine knew it. As long as he didn't go into the cell, it would work until they changed both codes like they did every evening. It wasn't a big change, although it did make things a bit more complicated.

And Bayard had no idea what to do with Percival now. Could he still try to convince Percival to change sides? Maybe he could appeal to him on what the conclave would do to Percival if they found out about this. Even though Percival knew, hearing it from someone else could push him in the right direction.

"He could still take a hostage," Mordred pointed out.

"Not unless I go inside," Amyas intervened.

"You can't be the only one to bring him food and keep an eye on him. That's why we have four guards assigned to him."

"It wouldn't have to be just me. The ability the sirens have is sexual."

Bayard blinked. "What do you mean?"

"Exactly what I said. Percival can't compel me because I'm an undine, but he also wouldn't be able to compel a lesbian, for example. I'm not sure how it works, since I'm not a siren, but from what I know, they use sexuality and physical attraction to compel. That means that if you send in a straight guy, a lesbian, or even an asexual person, he shouldn't be able to use his ability."

Maybe that was part of the reason the conclave didn't

know about this. Bayard couldn't help but wonder what good an ability that worked that way was. Not that it mattered. It just meant they had a way to keep an eye on Percival without anyone being compelled to do something they didn't want, which was what they'd been trying to find.

"And you're sure about that?" Mordred asked.

"As sure as I can be. I could contact someone to ask more about the sirens' ability, but I don't think you want people to know why I'm asking."

"I don't. We need to keep this as quiet as possible."

Amyas nodded. "That's what I thought. It's not going to be easy, since a lot of the people here are fluid when it comes to their sexuality, but if everything else fails, I can do it."

Amyas was right, but that didn't mean every fallen hero would be attracted to Percival. It was true that being immortal meant heroes had a long time to experiment when it came to sex and attraction. The conclave didn't allow it, but when heroes left the conclave, almost all of them had a period of time where they slept with everything that moved. Bayard had gone through it, and he wasn't the only one. Some realized they only like the opposite sex after that, while some, like Amyas had said, were more fluid. Bayard had always known he liked males more, even though he also enjoyed sex with women.

That made him the perfect target for Percival's ability. He probably shouldn't go back in that cell, but he'd never been afraid of taking risks.

He got to his feet. "I want to talk to him first."

Mordred sighed as if he'd expected that. "You realize he's going to try to compel you."

Bayard grinned. "He can try. We'll see if he manages."

"And if he does?"

"Then I hope you'll drag me out of that room before I can do something stupid."

53

Percival stared at the wall and waited for doom. Something was about to happen, but he didn't know what or how to prepare for it. The fallen heroes knew he was part siren, and if they were smart—and unfortunately, they were—they'd use it against him. He didn't know how they would, but it probably included threatening to tell the conclave if he didn't give them the information they wanted.

Because that was one of their goals. In the beginning, Percival hadn't believed they wanted to convince him to pass over to their side, but they did. They also wanted information, and having Percival on their side would make it easier to obtain it. Now, they wouldn't have to convince him of anything. They just had to threaten to contact the conclave and tell them what Percival was, and he might tell them everything.

He wasn't sure he would. He didn't want to lose the conclave or to be killed, but his job was to protect humanity and the conclave. He couldn't give the fallen heroes the information they wanted. He couldn't betray the conclave, no matter what happened to him.

He wasn't surprised when he heard footsteps coming closer. He expected it to be Amyas again, since they had to know that Percival would be able to compel pretty much any other person that came close to him. Maybe it would be a good thing. Amyas was far from being a fighter, and while Percival couldn't compel him, he could take him hostage and use him to get out of here.

The door opened. Amyas appeared, and Percival straightened in his chair. Amyas didn't come in, though. Instead, he moved to the side, and Bayard stepped into the room. He looked at Amyas instead of Percival. "Make sure it's locked," he ordered.

"I will. I'll keep an eye on you, too."

Bayard nodded. "And if he takes me hostage, don't give him anything."

"I'm not sure Mordred will be okay with that, but all right."

Amyas closed the door, and Percival heard the beeping of him locking it. He could feel Bayard's gaze on him, but he was afraid of looking up. He didn't even know why. What did it matter what Bayard or any other fallen heroes thought of him? They were traitors.

But Bayard knew what Percival could do now. He would use it against Percival, and for that, Percival was ready. What he wasn't ready for was for anyone to know what he was.

He'd kept it a secret for hundreds of years. Even before, the only person who'd known was his father, and having someone else aware of it made Percival feel vulnerable. It wasn't a sensation he enjoyed, and he wanted to get rid of it. Unfortunately, the only thing he could do was face whatever was about to happen.

So he looked up, looking at Bayard straight in the eyes. "What do you want?"

Bayard leaned against the wall, crossing his arms over his chest. "I'd like to know how you managed to hide that you're half siren from the conclave for so long."

Percival had been aware he knew, but it was still a hit to hear Bayard say the words out loud. Percival's first instinct was to deny. "I'm not part siren. I wouldn't be a hero if I were."

Bayard didn't seem to mind that Percival was contradicting him. "That's why I'm so impressed. You managed to hide that you're part supernatural for hundreds of years. How did you do it? Is it as simple as not using your ability, or is there more to it?"

Percival's instinct was still to deny, deny, deny. "There's nothing to hide because I'm a hero. I've worked for the conclave for hundreds of years. They trust me."

"I highly doubt that. The conclave doesn't trust anyone, not even other conclave members. Besides, you're young for a hero. You might have been one for hundreds of years, but that's still nothing next to how long some of the heroes have been with the conclave. Take Mordred, for example. He was a hero for almost a thousand years. How's that for experience?"

Percival had met heroes who'd worked for the conclave for so long, but rarely. Usually, they ended up being part of the conclave sooner or later. If they didn't, they just disappeared. Percival had always thought they'd retired, but now he wondered instead whether they'd started working for Mordred.

Bayard was older than Percival, but younger than Mordred. That was the only thing Percival was sure of, and while he wanted to ask, he didn't dare. He also didn't care, or at least, that was what he was trying to convince himself.

"Let's get back to you," Bayard said. "Who was a siren in your family? I'm thinking your mother, since we weren't able to find out anything about her, while we know a bit more about your father."

Percival shot to his feet. "Leave my father out of this," he snapped.

Bayard arched a brow. "Your father has been dead for a long time."

The protectiveness didn't make sense if Percival thought about it, but his father had always protected him, and he wanted to do the same, even though his father had been dead for a long time. But he'd been the only one who'd supported Percival, and that wasn't something Percival could forget easily — or at all.

"Let's assume it was your mother," Bayard continued. "Your father was human, right?"

Percival wouldn't answer even one question. It was bad enough that Bayard knew what he was and that his mother was a siren. Answering any question would make the situation even worse, and that wasn't something Percival could afford. He still had hope that eventually he'd escape. He'd have to go back to the conclave when he did, and that wouldn't be possible if Bayard contacted them with information about him.

Percival sat down again, crossing his arms over his chest. He hoped Bayard would take the hint, but instead, he continued talking and asking questions.

"All right, so you don't want to talk about your parents. Why don't you tell me how you managed to keep this a secret from the conclave for so long?"

That question made Percival hesitate. Maybe if he told Bayard about his pills, the fallen hero could find him some.

But no. Why would he, when if he didn't give them to Percival, it would be easier to expose him for what he was? Percival was already vulnerable enough in this situation. He had to be careful and protect himself.

"You know what I don't understand?" Bayard asked. "You know what the conclave thinks about supernatural creatures. We both do. You were raised the same way I was. Besides, they send you out to kill supernatural creatures, maybe even sirens. How can you do that to your brethren?"

Percival gritted his teeth. "They're not my brethren. The heroes are."

"The heroes would gladly kill you if they ever found out what you are. Why do you continue working for the conclave? You know what they'd do to you if they found out about this. Why are you so ready to sacrifice yourself for people who don't deserve it and who don't give a shit about you?"

Percival tightened his hands into fists, squeezing so hard his nails dug into his palms. "The conclave does what they were created for. They protect humanity from supernatural creatures, from monsters who hurt it."

"Are you a monster, then?" Bayard asked in a whisper.

Percival didn't know how to answer that. He always did his best not to think about what he was, but when he couldn't deny or ignore it, he had to admit that maybe, there *was* a monster inside of him. Maybe the conclave should kill him. So far, he hadn't hurt anyone he hadn't been ordered to kill, but maybe one day his siren half would take over.

"Maybe I am," he answered in the same tone.

CHAPTER FIVE

Bayard had a plan. It would probably be a disaster like his plans often were, but this time, he had faith. He couldn't *not*, not when the only other alternative was to kill Percival.

Percival was a study in contradictions. He was a hero, yet he was also a supernatural creature. He was aware of what he was, yet he continued working for the conclave. Bayard was surprised Percival's brain hadn't exploded yet, and he wanted to help him more than ever.

Bayard could never understand how Percival felt, working for the conclave when the conclave would gladly kill him. He didn't think he could wrap his mind around that, but he wanted Percival to open his eyes. What the conclave was doing was wrong. Percival wasn't a monster, no matter what he was convinced of, and he should be able to live his life openly instead of hiding what he was.

He wasn't the first hero who was part supernatural creature, although as far as Bayard knew, he was the only one still working for the conclave. Sometimes, abilities didn't manifest themselves until something triggered them, especially if instead of parents, a grandparent was a supernatural creature. Some heroes managed to hide what they were for a while, but they usually left the conclave.

Percival hadn't, and he wasn't planning on doing so anytime soon, as far as Bayard understood. He didn't accept what he was, and that was Bayard's first main goal. He would get Percival to see that being half siren wasn't a bad thing and that no, he wasn't a monster, no matter what the conclave had told him. Hopefully, that would be the first step to accepting himself and finally seeing what the conclave was doing, and Percival would move to their side.

The fallen heroes worked with supernatural creatures all the time. Hell, Mordred was dating one. They didn't care that Percival was half siren, and they wouldn't hold it against him or kill him for it.

And as far as Bayard could see, the only way to make Percival understand and accept that was to spend time with him and show him he truly didn't care what Percival was. That could be dangerous if Percival decided to use his ability on Bayard, but the thing with the two codes they'd come up with was working, and Bayard had every intention of using it. He'd get the guards to lock him into Percival's cell, and if Percival tried to hurt him, well, he'd deal with that if the time came. He had a lot more experience than Percival, and he was positive he could defend himself if Percival attacked him.

Bayard whistled as he walked down the hallway that led to the cell. He knew Percival could hear him and that he was annoying him. He peeked through the window in the door before unlocking it, and sure enough, Percival looked grumpy.

Bayard turned to Bowen. "Make sure to lock the door once I'm in."

"Of course." Bowen hesitated. "Are you sure you don't want me to stay out here?"

"There's no need for you to. Whatever Percival decides to do, I can deal with it."

"He could compel you to stay still while he kills you."

"He could, but what would he gain doing that? I'd be dead, and you guys would be angrier than ever. He knows there's no way he'd be let go if he did that."

Bowen still didn't look convinced, but he nodded. Bayard slipped into the room and waited for Bowen to lock it. He grinned at Percival. "We're locked inside now."

"I have ears," Percival grumbled. "I heard the lock."

"Someone is grumpy this morning. What did you do last night?"

Percival was sitting cross-legged on the bed and not looking at Bayard. Bayard couldn't be a hundred percent sure, but Percival looked more vulnerable than he had earlier. He wasn't as well put together as usual when Bayard visited him. His blond hair — and he really needed a haircut — was all over the place, as if he'd just woken up, or maybe because he'd raked his hands through it. He looked like he hadn't slept much, and Bayard was sorry about that. He'd done what he could to reassure Percival they wouldn't kill him, but he could tell Percival didn't believe him, and he couldn't blame him for that.

If Bayard's goal hadn't been to get Percival to move to their side and help them against the conclave, he wouldn't hesitate to use what he now knew about Percival against him. He could threaten to contact the conclave and tell them what Percival was if he didn't give them the information they wanted. It would be the easiest way to ruin Percival's life and everything he'd built until now.

Bayard wasn't planning to do that, though. He and Mordred had talked, and they felt it was more important than ever to make Percival see what the conclave was doing. Who better than he could understand how dangerous the conclave was? Who could be better proof of how cruel the conclave was when they would kill him if they ever found out what he was?

But before Percival agreed to help them, Bayard would have to convince him to accept himself. Talk about an easy job.

Since Percival was sitting on the bed, Bayard took one of the chairs, turned it around, and straddled it. He stared at Percival, trying to find something to say. "Are you going to try to convince me to let you go?" he eventually asked.

"Why should I do that when I know it won't work?"

Bayard nodded. He'd expected that answer. "You want me to check your knuckles?"

"No."

Bayard sighed. He'd expected that, too, but he didn't have to like it.

He suspected that reminding Percival of who he was and of his father was the best way to get through his shell, but to do that, Bayard would have to expose himself. He'd thought about it, and he was ready to do it. He just hoped it would work.

He crossed his forearms on the back of the chair and leaned in. "I already told you I was taken when I was seventeen," he began.

Percival's gaze flickered to Bayard, but he didn't say anything.

"My family was shocked when I went back," Bayard continued. "They had a hard time believing what I was telling them about the conclave, but eventually, they did. They wanted me to stay with them, but it was impossible. If the conclave had found out, they wouldn't have hesitated to kill my parents. I knew that about them even back then, and I was right. They wouldn't have wanted me to have anything beyond them, and I would have lost my family if they'd found out."

"Why are you telling me this?" Percival asked.

Bayard shrugged. "Because you're not talking, and I don't like silence. Anyway, once I went back to the conclave, I continued visiting my family. I helped them as much as I could and protected them, and my parents had a long and happy life. I think it helped them to know that I was okay."

Bayard hesitated. The next bit was something not a lot of people knew and could possibly get his family in trouble, but he suspected the best way for Percival to realize how similar they were and that the conclave was wrong was to offer a piece of himself.

"I kept in contact with my family even after my parents died. I continued visiting my siblings, and then when they were gone, too, their children and grandchildren. I'm in contact with them even now."

That got Percival's attention. "But your siblings have been dead a long time."

"They have. The people who descended from them are still my family, though. They're important, no matter what the conclave thinks. I wouldn't give them up for anything. They're my past and my future, part of who I am, and I'm not ashamed of them."

Bayard didn't understand. Percival wasn't ashamed of what he was — he was terrified.

All his life, he'd been told that supernatural creatures were monsters. He could only imagine what he might be able to do if he let his siren half surface, and he couldn't allow it to take control. He'd been willing to use it if it meant freeing himself, but now that Bayard and the others knew what he was, they'd be more careful, and that wouldn't be possible.

But he wanted to give in. He wanted to talk to Bayard, to admit he was terrified. He was lonely. He'd never been a people person, and he didn't really have friends, just colleagues and team members, but being stuck in a cell for a month was wearing on him. He wanted to talk to someone, even if that someone was Bayard.

He couldn't give in. If he did, the fallen heroes might tell the conclave, and the conclave wouldn't take him back. They'd hunt and kill him, and he'd lose everything.

The problem was that some of what Bayard said made

sense, if Percival allowed himself to think about it. Bayard was unique in the sense that even though he was a hero, he had a family and people he trusted. Percy couldn't imagine that. The only person he'd ever trusted was his father, and he was long dead. They'd lost years together because of the conclave, but Percival couldn't get angry at the conclave. They'd taken him away from his father for a reason, and he still believed in that reason.

But it hurt. He wanted what Bayard had. He wanted his father back and people he could trust and not have to think about what he could or couldn't say when he was around them. How would that feel? Percival didn't know because he'd never had that, and he didn't think he ever would.

And now that the fallen heroes knew what Percival was, he couldn't avoid thinking about what the conclave would have done to him in their place. The fallen heroes hadn't tortured him. They'd kept him prisoner, yes, but he was in a comfortable room, and he was given plenty of food and even medical attention after he'd punched the wall. The conclave, on the other hand, wouldn't have hesitated to torture him. They wouldn't have cared, especially once they'd found out he was part siren. Even before that, though, they'd have hurt him without thinking twice about it. It was what they did to get the answers they needed, and it didn't matter if the people they tortured were supernatural creatures or heroes.

They didn't torture heroes often. Most heroes stayed in line and did what the conclave wanted. One step out of line, and the conclave didn't hesitate. They couldn't afford to. They had to show every single hero that they were in charge and would act accordingly if the warriors didn't obey. Percival had seen it more times than he was comfortable with, and he'd promised himself he'd never be in that position.

And now he was. Because even if the fallen heroes freed him or if he somehow managed to escape, the conclave wouldn't welcome him with open arms. They'd want to know what happened to him and what he'd told the fallen heroes. They wouldn't believe his promises that he hadn't said anything. They'd torture him to know the truth, and he couldn't ignore that knowledge anymore.

He was having a hard time reconciling those two sides of the conclave. They were still fighting a fight Percival believed in. He wanted to protect humanity, and he'd do everything he could to accomplish that. He'd followed conclave orders for hundreds of years, never thinking twice about them, because the conclave knew what they were doing. It had been created thousands of years ago and had been protecting humans ever since.

But the conclave was also cruel and violent. They didn't hesitate to torture people, be they supernatural creatures or heroes. Percival didn't have to think back far to come up with names of heroes who'd disappeared after the conclave hadn't been happy with them. The last one had managed to escape right before they were to execute him, but he was one of the few lucky ones.

Nothing in this situation was easy or understandable. Percival couldn't ignore the dark side of the conclave anymore, not when his siren half was emerging, but what was he supposed to do? He still believed in the conclave's mission, even though he wasn't sure he believed in them.

"Percival?"

Percival shook his head. He didn't know if Bayard had continued talking to him. He'd been lost in his thoughts, which was dangerous in his situation. "What?" he snapped.

"I just wanted to be sure you were okay. I lost you for a bit there."

Percival didn't want to show that he was changing his mind. He wasn't even sure he was. "You said you still have contact with your family," he said to distract Bayard.

Bayard blinked but nodded. "I do."

"How? I don't know how old you are exactly, but you have to be almost as old as Mordred, and he's thousands of years old. How do you hide that from your family?"

Bayard shrugged. "They know there's something strange about me. They know I don't age or die. A few asked about it, and I've told them what I could, but most just view me as an old uncle and are more than happy to keep my secret. I suppose it makes sense for them. If I can, I help them, both financially and with anything else they need. They know that as long as I'm around, they're safe. I suppose they also know what would happen if anyone from the human government found out about me. They don't want that, so they keep me safe, and I keep them safe."

Percival hadn't thought he wanted a family. After losing his father, he'd closed himself off, and he'd continued doing so for close to three hundred years. It had been easy because none of the heroes working for the conclave wanted to be close to him. Everyone was more than happy to focus on the work, especially when the conclave tightly controlled friendships and relationships between heroes.

But that wasn't what had happened here. Here, the fallen heroes were friends. They were family.

And for the first time in almost three hundred years, Percival yearned for that.

Bayard could see Percival was softening—or that something was changing in him, anyway. Hopefully, it meant Percival would move to their side, but at the moment, that wasn't what Bayard was focused on.

He remembered all too well how cruel and hard the conclave could be. It wasn't just that they'd happily kill Percival if they found out what he was. It was also that the conclave wanted absolute control over heroes, and that meant no relationships that the conclave didn't approve of. Since they didn't approve of any kind of relationship, being a hero was a lonely job.

It was necessary. The conclave couldn't afford for heroes to have someone more important than them. If a hero had to choose between the conclave and someone they loved, they wouldn't even have to think twice about it, except maybe when it came to people like Percival, who were blindly loyal. Even Percival wasn't anymore, though. No matter how much he protested, Bayard could see it.

The conclave forbid relationships, even friendships between heroes. Since all heroes were supposed to live in the same building where the conclave was based, it was easy to keep an eye on them and make sure they didn't have anyone.

It was lonely. That was one of the things Bayard remembered well from the time he'd been a hero. He'd watched the other heroes he was friendly with harden or die—neither had appealed to him. And when Mordred had contacted him, he'd been more than happy to leave the conclave behind. He hadn't regretted it yet, and he didn't think he ever would.

But now that Percival was finally giving in, at least in part, Bayard had something up his sleeve he could finally use.

No one knew about it, not even Mordred, who'd kick his ass if he found out. Bayard had been clear with Cecil when the mage had helped him with the spell. He didn't want anyone to know, and he'd be the one to tell Mordred about this. It would be better for Mordred to forgive him than to say no, which was why Bayard hadn't mentioned it.

It was the right thing to do. Even though Percival was finally coming to accept what the conclave would do to him if they found out what he was, he was still loyal to them. Now that he had doubts, this was the best moment for Bayard to hammer that in and to show Percival the kind of life he could have if he decided to switch sides.

Bayard straightened and looked at Percival. "I have an offer."

Percival looked wary. "What offer?"

"I'm sure you know by now, the fallen heroes, as you call us, work with supernatural creatures. That includes a mage."

"And? Or did you tell me that just so that I knew I'd be killed if I tried to escape?"

"You might not want to continue to try to escape after you hear what I have to say."

"By all means. I'm listening."

Bayard grinned. He liked it when Percival listened to what he had to say and thought about it, but he much preferred this side of Percival. He wasn't quite as beaten-down and sad as he'd been before, and Bayard wanted that to continue. "All right, Percy. Listen to me, and listen well."

Percival grimaced. "My name isn't Percy. It's Percival."

"I like Percy better." And Bayard hoped that if they became friends, he'd be allowed to call him that.

Percival scowled. "If you call me Percy, I'll call you Bay."

Bayard didn't have a problem with that. "All right. You can call me Bay."

"I never said I *wanted* to call you that," Percy protested, but Bay was already focused on the next part of his plan.

"As I was saying, we have a mage here. I asked him to create a spell that would link you and me together."

Percy blinked. "What does that mean?"

"Exactly what I said. If we use the spell, we won't be able to move far from each other. Also, everything that happens to one of us will happen to the other. That means that you won't be able to escape or hurt me."

Cecil had enjoyed the creation of the spell, but he'd also been worried. He'd never done anything like this, and he'd made sure to warn Bay that there might be some problems and things he couldn't anticipate. It was a risk to use the spell, but Bay wasn't changing his mind. He wanted to show Percy how his life could be if he let go of his loyalty for the conclave and finally accepted what the conclave was.

"Why would you do something like that?" Percy asked.

Bay took two bracelets out of his pocket. "Because you've been here for a month, and you still haven't changed your mind. Things have changed, and I think that giving you a chance at a normal life might help you see the reality of the conclave and that the fallen heroes aren't bad people. It's your one chance to be allowed out of the cell."

Percy's eyes narrowed. "You mean that if I put that on, you'll show me around the house? Or will you let me go?"

Bay shook his head. "Not let you go, no. From what Cecil said, you'll be able to be sixteen feet away from me, nothing more. And of course, you won't be able to attack me, because you'd get hurt, too. You should consider yourself lucky. This has never been done before for any hero we've captured."

Percy stared at the bracelets. Bay already knew his answer would be yes, but he was still worried. He felt better when Percy nodded and held an arm out.

"You're sure this will work?" Percy asked.

"It will. Cecil is a great mage, and he promised it would." He'd also warned Bayard some things could go awry, but Bay didn't want to worry about that now.

"Since this is the only way out of the cell, let's do it," Percy said.

Bay snapped the bracelet around Percy's wrist. Nothing happened, but then, he wasn't wearing his yet.

The bracelets were simple silver, and they would be stuck on their wrists until Cecil himself took them off. That was one more thing Bay had insisted on. He didn't want Percy to be able to take it off and run away.

He held Percy's gaze as he put the bracelet on his wrist, too.

Then, they waited.

"What's supposed to happen?" Percy asked in a whisper.

"I don't know. It's the first time Cecil's done something like this. He couldn't tell me."

"I suppose you should try leaving the cell and see if you reach sixteen feet."

Bay considered Percy. Was this something he was saying to try to escape? But Bay trusted him with this. He would have to take Percy out of the cell if the spell worked, so he might as well try now.

He got to his feet and walked to the door. He knocked, then had to wait a few moments for someone to open. Bowen's face appeared at the window. He looked relieved, at least until he opened the door and Bay ordered him to keep it open.

"What about the prisoner?" he asked.

"If things worked the way they were supposed to do, he'll be out of here soon anyway," Bay explained.

Bowen gaped, but Bay ignored him and tried walking away.

He couldn't. He couldn't even cross the doorstep. It was as if there was a wall in front of him, and every time he tried taking a step forward, he was pulled back toward Percy.

He turned around. "How much distance do you think is between us right now?" he asked.

Percy looked like he wanted to kill him. "About six feet. Why?"

"Well, Cecil warned me that something like this might happen. It's the first time he's used this kind of spell, and he couldn't make any promises. He did say that the distance would be a tricky thing, and he was right. I think the maximum distance we can be apart is this."

Which would make things interesting to say the least.

Percy wanted to kill Bay, but now that they had the bracelets on, he couldn't do it without hurting himself, too. Still, the urge was strong, so he pushed his hands under his thighs and glared at Bay. "You said sixteen feet," he said through gritted teeth.

Bay didn't seem bothered by the difference. "So we'll have to stay closer than we expected. I don't see how that will be a problem."

"You don't? Six feet means we'll have to stay in the same room all the time." And that included the bathroom. Well, maybe not, depending on how big the bathroom was, but they'd still have to stay embarrassingly close to each other as they used it, and Percy did *not* want to think about that right now.

Bay shrugged. "So? You lived with the conclave until recently. I'm sure you're used to sharing personal space with other heroes. I promise I won't tell people you snore, if that's what you're worried about."

Yep. Percy would eventually end up hurting himself just because he wanted to kill Bay.

He got to his feet. The guard who'd opened the door, Bowen, took a step forward and reached for the knife at his waist. Percy stopped moving. Even though Bay had promised he'd be allowed out of here and would have to keep that promise because of the bracelets, it didn't mean everyone would be happy.

But they wouldn't be able to hurt Percy.

Percy hadn't thought about that aspect, but this was dangerous for Bay. If one of the fallen heroes wanted to kill Percy, they wouldn't be able to because they'd hurt Bay right along with him. Was that something Bay had thought about, or had he only focused on Percy not hurting him?

"We should probably talk to Cecil, though," Bay continued.

Percy crossed his arms over his chest so he wouldn't try to strangle Bay just yet. "You think?"

Bay grinned. "Well, he wanted to talk to us anyway after we put the bracelets on. Come on. Let's go."

He stepped out of the room but couldn't go any further. Percy took a step toward him, then another. He walked past Bowen, who was glaring at him.

Percy didn't trust anyone, not even Bay. He shouldn't have trusted the spell, not when mages were supernatural creatures. But this was his only way out of the cell, and he hadn't been able to say no. He didn't care about the house or getting to know more fallen heroes. He just cared about getting out of that cell before he went nuts.

He followed Bay down the hallway. They reached another door, and Bay knocked on the window like he had when they'd been in the cell. A face appeared, and Constantine beamed.

Percy groaned. He did *not* want to face Constantine at the moment. The man was too happy for his own good on the best of days, and if Percy knew anything about him, he'd be delighted Percy was out of the cell. He'd probably try to become his best friend or something like that, and the thought exhausted Percy.

The door swung open. "You're out of your cell," Constantine exclaimed.

Percy glared at him. "For now."

"It means you're one of us now."

"Not quite," Bay intervened. "But he's not going anywhere, and he won't hurt me, so you don't have to worry. We're just going to find Cecil."

They moved toward the door, and once again, Percy followed him. This door led to a set of stairs that they climbed. When Bay opened the next door, sunlight flooded the area, and Percy had to close his eyes for a moment.

He hadn't seen sunlight in a month. He felt like if he stepped into the sun, he'd burn to a crisp like a vampire, even though that was impossible. He sucked in a breath, then followed Bay through the door.

He'd thought many times about the place he was in. He hadn't been sure if it was a small jail the fallen heroes had put together or another place, but he hadn't expected it to be j under what was obviously their home.

Everything around him was beautiful. The house was huge, which made him wonder if all the fallen heroes lived here. There was carpet on the floor, art on the walls, and wide windows that allowed Percy to see lush gardens.

He pinched himself, unable to believe what he was seeing.

Bay yelped.

Percy frowned, then understood what had happened. "You really feel everything I feel?" he asked. He pinched himself again, just to try.

Bay reached out and slapped the back of Percy's head. It didn't hurt, but Bay groaned anyway. "I shouldn't have done that," Bay muttered. "And yes, I do feel everything you feel, so stop pinching yourself. Come on. Cecil said he'd be waiting in the kitchen. We can talk to Mordred later."

Percy wasn't sure what to make of the fact that Bay hadn't consulted his boss before doing this. Did that mean no one in the house knew Percy was free? What would happen if someone saw him and decided to attack him? They might not have time to warn them that hurting Percy would mean hurting Bay, too, if they did.

But Percy was out of the cell. That was what he wanted to focus on. He followed Bay down the hallway, unable to stop looking around.

Under the carpets, the floors were dark wood. It should have made the hallway dark, but there was plenty of light coming through the windows. They walked past several doors, but Percy didn't stop. He couldn't, not when Bay was still walking straight ahead. After a few minutes, the house felt like a maze.

"Here we are," Bay eventually said. He walked through an open doorway, right into the kitchen.

Once again, there were wide windows on the other side of the room. The kitchen furniture was dark wood like the floor, while the counters were marble. Percy closed his eyes and let the sunlight play on his face. God, he'd missed this. He wanted so much more, but he was afraid to ask. He was afraid to push too much and for even this to be taken away from him.

"What is he doing here?" a voice asked.

Percy opened his eyes, wondering why he'd closed them when he knew he was in enemy territory.

Two men were sitting at the kitchen island. Percy didn't know either of them, but he instantly recognized the mage. The red eyes were a dead giveaway, although they weren't as creepy as he'd expected, especially with the longish brown curls that topped the mage's head. They made him look softer, and Percy felt himself relax without meaning to.

The mage was pale and slightly pudgy. It wasn't a bad look on him, and if the way the other man had wrapped an arm around the mage's waist was anything to go by, he'd found someone who appreciated it.

The other man made all of Percy's instincts go wild. He narrowed his eyes, trying to understand what the man was. He was tall, blond, and broad. There was a ring in his lip, and when Percy discreetly sniffed, he could smell earth and forest. A draugr, then. Percy wasn't even surprised that the fallen heroes worked with supernatural creatures. He wasn't happy about it, but he kept his mouth shut.

"I used the bracelets," Bay said, raising his wrist.

The mage's eyes widened. "Did they work?"

"You gave those to him without knowing whether or not they would work?" Percy asked.

The draugr looked like he wanted to hit Percy, and Percy didn't blame him. He needed to keep these people on his good side. Eventually, he'd get rid of the bracelet and would be able to leave. Until then, Bay had to believe he was more than happy to go along with this.

And he was.

Bay slid onto a stool on the other side of the kitchen island. "They do, but instead of the sixteen feet you talked about, we can't be apart more than six or seven feet."

The mage grimaced. "I warned you something like that could happen."

"As far as I can see, it's the only problem, so that's good."

Percy sighed. Bay didn't seem to mind any of this, and he supposed he didn't, either. He was free of his cell. He would have to spend time with fallen heroes and supernatural creatures, but it would give him the opportunity to gather information. He still hadn't given up trying to go back to the conclave, although before that happened, he'd have to find his pills. There was no way he could go back when his siren half was so close to emerging.

"What's going on here?" a voice boomed behind them.

Percy sighed and turned around to face Mordred.

CHAPTER SIX

"What were you thinking?" Mordred hissed.

Bay ignored him and kept his attention on Percy, who was on his other side. They were sitting at the table in the dining room, having dinner with the other fallen heroes present in the house. Percy's eyes were wide, and he was watching everyone and barely talking. Bay wasn't surprised. After the fight the two of them had with Mordred, Percy had closed off, and even though Bay was angry, he understood where Mordred was coming from.

"I can't believe you did something so stupid," Mordred added.

Bay sighed and turned to him. "I had to do something. He'd already been in the cell a month. How much longer would you have let him stay?"

Mordred shook his head. "You shackled yourself to him. What's going to happen if he tries to run?"

"We already talked about that. He won't be able to, because he can't move away from me more than six feet. Cecil promised everything else is as it should be. Why don't you trust me? You put me in charge of this, and I'm trying to do my job."

"I put you in charge of convincing him to see the conclave for what they are, not of shackling yourself to him."

Bay peeked at Percy, but he was focused on his plate. "I knew what I was doing when I put that bracelet on," he told Mordred. They'd already had this conversation, but apparently, it wasn't over yet. "Cecil and I talked before I did. I told him what I was looking for, and he explained what his doubts were and how the spell could misfire. I knew all of that, yet I decided to do it anyway."

"I could remove it," Cecil offered from the other side of the table.

Percy dropped his fork, and the sound of it hitting the porcelain of his plate made half the table look at him. He kept his gaze on Cecil. "You can't do that."

Cecil grimaced. "I understand where you're coming from, but while I expected it to have a few small problems, the distance thing is kind of big. Do you really want to have to spend the next week sleeping in Bay's bed?"

Percy's eyes widened.

That was something Bay hadn't thought about, but he didn't mind.

"I don't care where I have to sleep. You can't get rid of the spell."

Percy was starting to panic, and Bay could understand why. He'd been stuck in that cell for a month. It would have driven anyone nuts, but Percy had resisted more than Bay had expected. Even if they didn't manage to convince him to pass to their side, he deserved a little freedom. Besides, Bay was still convinced this was the right thing to do. Keeping Percy in his cell and talking to him hadn't worked. This would. He was sure of it.

"Just try to fix it," he told Cecil. "You don't have to get rid of it."

Cecil bit his lower lip and nodded. "I'll do my best, but I can't make any promises."

"We don't expect you to. Anything you can come up with will be fine."

Mordred was still grumbling, but thankfully, he didn't intervene. Everyone went back to their food, for which Bay was relieved. He leaned closer to Percy, intent on asking him how he was doing, but before he could, someone at the table asked, "What's the conclave up to now?"

That got Percy's attention. He didn't look up, but Bay saw it.

Mordred sighed. "They're not happy," he said. "They tried contacting me a few times, but I doubt they have anything new to tell me. They found out about the message I sent the heroes."

"Hopefully, that message will be enough to let the heroes know they have a safe place if they need one," Sybil said.

"A few have already reached out for help leaving the conclave," Mordred confirmed.

Percy sucked in a breath.

Bay was glad when no one seemed to notice, but this was why he'd wanted to take Percy out of his cell. Listening to this, hearing what the conclave had done to its heroes, could be enough to finish changing his mind.

"What did the conclave do to them?" Bay asked. He knew what he was doing, and from the way Mordred looked at him, he suspected Mordred did, too.

"One of them lost her entire family to the conclave. She tried going back, but we all know how the conclave reacts to that kind of behavior. As far as I know, the only one who managed is Bay. As for Laila's family, when the conclave found she'd gone back, they killed all of them."

Bay peeked at Percy. Percy was staring at his roasted chicken, but he wasn't eating anymore. He seemed frozen.

"That sounds like your story, Bowen," Bay said quietly.

Bowen glared, but he also nodded curtly. "I didn't even try to go back," he spat out. "They killed my family because my parents came too close to finding me."

"I know what you're doing," Percy said in a whisper.

"Do you? Because I'm sure you already knew all these stories. Heroes might not be allowed to become friends, but it doesn't mean we don't talk to each other. Tell me you didn't know."

Percy couldn't because he *had* known. All the heroes knew about these stories. They weren't unique to Laila and Bowen. But when you were forced to work for the conclave, it was easier to ignore them. When you couldn't run away, you had to convince yourself that the conclave was doing the right thing.

"None of this is possible," Percy said.

Bay was grateful Bowen hadn't heard him. If he had, he would have tried to kill Percy. His family was a touchy subject, and Bay didn't blame him. "Of course it's possible. Stop hiding your head in the sand, Percy. You know this is what the conclave does. They take children from their parents. They lock them away, train them to be killers, kill them if they can't or won't obey. Before that, they use every trick they have, including killing entire families and villages so those children don't have anything to go back to. The conclave brainwashed all of us, including you. I can't force you to see it, but you have to admit that all of this does sound like the conclave."

Now that they'd started, other heroes were telling their stories. Everyone around the table already knew about this, but it felt good to talk about it sometimes. Bay usually stayed quiet, since he'd been able to protect his family. That wasn't even because he was particularly powerful or anything like that. The conclave had simply never found out he'd got back to his parents, but if they had, they *would* have killed Bay's entire family, just like they had with Bowen and Laila. Bay was lucky, and he knew it.

By the time everyone was done talking, Percy looked so pale that Bay was worried he might be about to faint. He'd stopped eating when they started talking, and his plate was still mostly full. Bay wanted him to eat more, but he wanted him to believe what had been said even more.

He leaned closer. "You heard what everyone here has to say about the conclave. Think about it. What would they do to you if they found out your mother was a siren?"

Percy's back went ramrod straight as he looked around, clearly panicked. Bay had made sure no one but him could hear his words, though. The fallen heroes around them wouldn't find out Percy was half siren from him. Percy would have to be the one to tell them if and when he wanted to.

"They'll kill you," he continued. "Because to them, you're a monster, no matter how much work you did or how many years you were loyal to them. They won't care about any of that if they find out about you. Is that really what you want? To sacrifice your life for someone who doesn't care about you? Who wouldn't hesitate to kill you for something you can't change?" They'd already had this conversation, but Bay hoped that after listening to the heroes around the table, Percy would finally be able to admit at least to himself that the conclave wasn't the perfection he'd thought they were until now.

Percy didn't want to think about any of this. He knew what the conclave did. He wasn't an idiot, and he wasn't blind. He'd been a hero for long enough to realize that what the conclave did wasn't always above board. It also wasn't always ethical, but as a hero, he'd obeyed the orders he was given. If he admitted that what the conclave did was wrong, then he'd have to admit he'd been wrong, too.

That would make *him* a monster, and he wasn't ready to face that yet.

But there was one thing he could agree with. He hadn't been happy with a lot of things the conclave had done over the years. He hadn't complained or tried to go against it because he hadn't thought it was a possibility. The fallen heroes had, and Percy admired them for that.

It was something he'd never have dared think a few days ago, let alone when he was still with the conclave. Even now, he was terrified that someone would realize and try to kill him. But he couldn't call everyone around the table a liar, and he'd seen many of those stories with his own two eyes. He'd never been sent to kill the family of a hero, not as far as he knew, but he couldn't deny that the possibility made him uncomfortable. He wanted answers, but he knew better than to ask them from the conclave.

The conclave was in charge, always. They didn't accept heroes going against their wishes and orders or even asking questions. When a hero did, it never ended well, which was why most didn't complain. That was why Percy hadn't. The conclave was all he'd had for close to three hundred years. What was he supposed to do?

He knew all of this, but he couldn't admit it to the people around the table. He couldn't admit to himself how wrong he'd been, so instead, he poked at his roasted chicken, trying to distract himself. He was relieved he was being left alone, even though he could feel gazes on him. Some fallen heroes were angry, and he wasn't sure he understood why. They'd been in this position before. They'd worked for the conclave, and someone had convinced them to leave. Well, Percy supposed it wasn't the same for all of them. Some had probably realized what was happening on their own and had found a way out.

He stayed silent through the rest of dinner and listened. He still had a hard time believing everything he was hearing, but he forced himself to consider the possibility that Bay was right and that the conclave wasn't the best thing for humanity. He'd had his doubts before, but it had been easy to push them away. Now, it was impossible.

"Why don't we go to my room?" Bay said as he rose from

his chair once dinner was over.

"Don't we have to help clean up?"

Bay looked surprised. "Are you offering?"

Percy shrugged. "If I'm going to live with you for any length of time, it's probably good I pull my own weight."

"I can't say I expected that, so thank you. You don't have to do it now. You've been through a lot over the past month, and I'm sure everyone will understand that you need rest away from that cell. By the way, do you need to go downstairs to grab anything?"

Percy never wanted to see the cell again, so he shook his head. "I'm fine. We can go."

He followed Bay out of the room — not that he had a choice. They were stuck together for as long as the bracelets were on their wrists, and Percy couldn't seem to get his off. He'd tried as discreetly as possible, but he was pretty sure Bay had noticed. He suspected the only person who could take them off was Cecil, and there was no way Percy would be able to convince him to do that. He didn't even think he'd be able to get close to Cecil, not as long as Cecil's boyfriend was with him.

Thor hadn't been rude or anything, but Percy had felt his gaze on him the entire time they'd been in the kitchen with Cecil and Mordred, and he knew the draugr wouldn't hesitate to kill him if he even as much as looked at Cecil the wrong way. Percy didn't understand that kind of feeling or protective instinct, but then, he supposed he'd never loved anyone the way Cecil and Thor loved each other.

"Bay!" Mordred called out.

Percy sighed. He'd hoped they were done with this, but apparently, they weren't. The conversation in the kitchen had mainly involved Mordred and Bay hissing at each other and being pissed, and Percy prayed this second conversation wouldn't devolve into more of that.

He and Bay turned to look at Mordred, who was striding

down the hallway to reach them.

"Before you go, I have rules," he declared.

Percy was surprised they hadn't done this before. He wanted to point out that he didn't exactly have a choice, since he couldn't go further away than six feet from Bay, but he didn't fancy being slammed against the wall and beaten up, so he kept his mouth shut.

Mordred glared at Percy. "You're a guest here. That means you won't threaten anyone. You won't be rude. You won't try to hurt anyone, not even one of the supernatural beings who live with us."

"I'm not an idiot," Percy snapped. "Not only is Bay stuck with me and would be able to hear anything I say, but some of your fallen heroes don't like me being here. If I as much as look at them or anyone else wrong, they won't hesitate to kill me, and I don't want that to happen. If there's one thing I can promise, it's that I won't hurt anyone." And he wouldn't try to escape, because he couldn't go anywhere unless he wanted to drag Bay with him, and he doubted he'd be able to do that.

To Percy's surprise, Mordred's expression softened. "Good. I know you're angry, and I understand. We kidnapped you and locked you up for a month, and that can't have been easy. I'd like for you to keep an open mind, though, the way you did at dinner. I understand that the conclave is all you know. It was for me for a long time, too, as it was for everyone here. But if you allow yourself to think about it, you'll see the conclave's true face."

"And if I do, I'll become one of you."

"You don't have to. Not all fallen heroes work with us. We'd like to welcome you here, but we understand that sometimes, it's not possible. It's up to you. We just have to be sure you won't run back to the conclave as soon as we let you go."

Which meant Percy would be stuck here for a while longer, especially if he continued being pigheaded and contradictory.

It would be much easier for him to lie and say he saw things the way Mordred and the others did, but he didn't want to do that.

He didn't want to do *any* of this. He couldn't face the truth when it came to the conclave, but now that his head had been pulled out of the sand — unwillingly — he couldn't put it back in. Eventually, he *would* have to face reality.

He just hoped he'd be ready for that when it happened and that it wouldn't break him.

Bay didn't mind sleeping in the same bed as Percy. He also wasn't afraid Percy would kill him in his sleep or anything like that. If he did, he'd be killing himself, and if there was one thing Percy didn't want, it was that.

For now, it seemed he was still planning to go back to the conclave if he could. Bay didn't know how else to get through to him, but he'd decided to give himself time. He and Percy had only been stuck together for a few hours, and those hours had been spent introducing Percy around and showing him part of the house. Hopefully, he'd settle down soon and would have time to think about the conclave and what they did.

Bay opened the door to his rooms and waved Percy inside. "Make yourself at home."

Percy snorted. "Not like I have a choice."

He looked more relaxed, which was good. Bay hoped they'd get to know each other now that Percy wasn't in his cell anymore. He also hoped they wouldn't have to execute Percy if he decided to go back to the conclave after all.

"I could take you back to your cell," Bay offered with a smile.

Percy shook his head and looked around. "That won't be necessary."

Bay had been living in his rooms for several decades. They were comfortable and exactly what he needed, but he tried seeing them in a new light, since Percy was.

Just like everywhere in the house, the windows were wide, so much so they took up almost the entire wall facing the lake. No one would be peeking in through them, and Bay enjoyed the sight.

The bed was right in front of the windows, separated from them only by a couple armchairs so Bay could watch outside without having to get up. There was a fireplace next to the windows on the left of the bed, and to the left of that was a small sitting area with more windows. Bay didn't spend as much time here as he wished he could, but maybe that would change once the conclave was taken care of.

He almost snorted at that thought. Once the conclave wasn't in place anymore, he and the others would have even more work, because they'd have to find a way to replace them.

Bay gestured at the doors that opened in his rooms. "That's the walk-in closet. We'll have to get your clothes from the cell so you can put them inside. The other door is the bathroom. There's both a tub and a shower."

Percy arched a brow. "It's not like I can use either of those, can I?"

"Why not?"

"Because we're stuck together."

"So? Haven't you ever seen a naked man?"

To Bay's delight, Percy's cheeks turned a light pink. He looked away, staring through the window. "Of course I have. I just don't want to take a bath with you standing right next to it."

"No baths, then. And we don't have to shower together, of course. We can take turns." Although Bay would have enjoyed sharing the shower with Percy. Percy wasn't here so

Bay could seduce him, and he had to keep that in mind. Maybe once Percy crossed to their side, they could revisit the idea.

Percy nodded curtly. "And I'll sleep on the floor."

Bay didn't mind showering separately, but this wasn't something he was willing to compromise on. "You'll sleep in the bed with me."

"I don't want to share your bed."

"I realize it might be awkward, but we're both adults. There's no need for you to sleep on the carpet."

"There's also no need for me to sleep in your bed."

Bay huffed. Percy had always been difficult, so he wasn't surprised he continued being so. "We should go back to your cell, then."

"You said you wouldn't ask Cecil to take the bracelets off."

"I won't. But maybe in the cell, you'll be more comfortable." Not that there was a second bed there, but Bay was trying to make Percy see how stupid this thing was. "And besides, there are other cells near the one you were in. I can sleep in the one next door." With as little space as there was in the cells, they'd still be six feet apart.

Percy stared at Bay. "Why would you offer to stay in my cell?"

"Why not? You're still a prisoner, but it doesn't mean you have to be uncomfortable. We're trying to lure you to our side, after all."

Percy rolled his eyes. "And you think telling me that is going to help?"

"Maybe not, but you already know what we're doing."

"Fine. We'll stay here, but I won't sleep in the bed."

Bay took a deep breath. Insisting was useless. Besides, Percy would soon realize the bed was more comfortable than the floor, and he'd move then. If he didn't, well, Bay was used to sleeping on his own. It wouldn't change anything for him.

"All right. We should use the bathroom."

Percy grimaced. "That's not going to be fun."

Bay agreed, but he decided to look at the bright side. It would be embarrassing and awkward, but it would also push Bay and Percy closer together. There was no way not to be friends after you had to be in the same room when someone used the bathroom.

They decided that the best way to do that was for one of them to shower while the other used the facilities. Bay was the first under the shower, and he took his time just to tease Percy. He regretted it when it was Percy's turn in the shower and he did the same. Bay couldn't feel Percy's hands on his own body, but he could feel the reaction happening in his groin, and he wasn't sure if it came from him or Percy. He also wasn't about to ask, so instead, he brushed his teeth and cleaned the area around the sinks.

Percy firmly avoided looking at Bay once he got out of the shower. That was fine with Bay, who didn't have the energy to do this anymore. He loaned Percy a pair of pajama pants and a soft t-shirt, and they went back to the bedroom. Bay didn't hesitate to get in bed, but Percy stood there, illuminated only by the moonlight, and stared down at him.

Bay sighed. "Look, if you really want, I can give you a pillow and a blanket, and you can sleep on the floor. You don't have to, though. I promise I'll keep my fallen hero hands away from you. We can even put some pillows between us to make sure we won't touch each other."

Percy looked like he wanted to accept, so Bay was surprised when he shook his head. "We don't have to put the pillows up. I trust you won't do anything."

Bay wasn't sure what that meant, but Percy was getting into bed with him, and that was what he'd been trying to make happen. He was too tired to examine Percy's decision or the way he felt. Instead, he closed his eyes and listened to

Percy raise the blankets and slide under them. He settled on the other side of the bed, as quiet and still as a dead body. Bay briefly considered telling him that, but he didn't want to start bickering.

Percy's breathing was soft and grew steadier as time passed. It was the first time in years Bay had shared the bed with someone, and while it was awkward, it was also reassuring and familiar. As he fell asleep, he couldn't help but wonder what it would be like if Percy shared his bed permanently.

CHAPTER SEVEN

When Percy woke up, he knew where he was. He also knew he had morning wood, and he was mortified.

He was on his back, and he stared at the ceiling, trying not to move and praying Bay was still asleep. He had to do something about this. He couldn't allow Bay to wake up and realize the state he was in.

He eyed the bathroom door, trying to judge the distance between it and the bed. Was it six feet or more? Could he manage to sneak in without Bay noticing? He had to take a cold shower, and he had to do it now.

"You're thinking so loudly I can hear it," Bay drawled.

Percy's heart raced. Bay was awake, so he had to know what Percy was feeling. Every time Percy moved, the blanket rubbed against his cock, and while he was doing his best to ignore it, he could *feel* it. That meant Bay could, too, which was why Percy was trying hard not to move.

Bay's face was pressed against the pillow, but he raised it and sleepily looked at Percy. "You know I have one of those, too, right?" he asked.

Percy couldn't look at him. "I have no idea what you're talking about."

Bay chuckled, shaking his head. "I don't understand why you should be ashamed or even try to hide it. I get that it's awkward, but really, you shouldn't focus on that. I'm pretty sure we're both in the same state, and it's not your fault. It's just morning."

Percy's face felt like it was on fire, and he wanted to die.

He couldn't listen to this anymore, so he shot out of bed, his legs tangling in the blankets. He almost fell on his face, but thankfully, he was trained, and he managed to scramble to his feet. He ran toward the bathroom, having every intention of slamming the door shut and hide for the rest of the day.

He never reached it. Before he could, pain seized his body, and he crumpled on the floor. He could hear Bay swear behind him and the soft sound of the blankets moving. The pain softened, then disappeared, and Percy felt Bay's hands on his shoulders.

"You have to be more careful." Bay gently touched Percy's chin to raise his face so they could look at each other. "I know this is awkward, embarrassing, and awful. I know you want none of this. Both of us are stuck unless you want to go back to your cell, and I know you don't. That means we have to learn to live together and to stay close to each other. I don't want you to get hurt."

Percy blinked. He pulled away, needing some space. He couldn't have more than six feet, but he could have a few inches. The problem was that he couldn't seem to forget how Bay's hands felt on him now that Bay had touched him.

Bay got to his feet. "I promise I won't tease you again. But really, there's nothing to be ashamed of. Both of us are males, and we're adults. Hell, we're immortal. We've lived long enough not to be embarrassed by morning wood."

Normally, Percy would agree with him. In this situation, though, he was entirely lost, and he didn't know how to deal with anything. Usually, when he was in a difficult situation, he fought his way out of it. He couldn't in this case, which meant he had no idea what to do.

Bay walked to the bathroom. Since Percy was still on the floor close to it, he was able to slip in and close the door. He didn't seem disturbed by what had just happened, and Percy didn't understand it. How could he do that? Yes, Percy understood they were stuck, and they weren't teenagers snickering over a boner, but still. He wasn't used to being so close to another person that they talked about morning wood.

He thought that said a lot about his life.

He hadn't been with anyone in longer than he could remember. Since the conclave didn't want heroes to have relationships, it was easier to stick with one-night stands. Besides, how was Percy supposed to explain to a human what he was and did? Since humans grew old and died, it wasn't worth it to be with them in the long term. The problem was that the only immortal supernatural beings other than heroes were creatures, so that was out, too. And since heroes couldn't be together, well, it didn't leave anyone for relationships.

But Mordred had found someone. He was dating Amyas, and both of them were immortal. They'd never have to leave each other. And Cecil and Thor were together, too. Neither of them was a hero, but they were happy.

Could Percy have that? Was that one of the things he could look forward to if he left the conclave? He didn't think he could ever have a relationship with a supernatural creature, but what about heroes? Of course, if he wanted to be with one, he'd have to be with a fallen hero, but that was what he would be, too.

The bathroom door opened, and Bay stepped out. He didn't look surprised to see Percy still on the floor, and he offered him a hand. When Percy didn't take it, Bay grinned.

"I washed my hands, if that's what you're wondering."

Percy looked away, but he finally took Bay's hand and allowed him to pull him to his feet.

"I'll sit in one of those armchairs while you're in the bathroom," Bay said. "They should be close enough that the distance won't give us problems."

Percy nodded and rushed into the bathroom, closing the door behind himself. He briefly leaned against it, trying to wrap his mind around what had just happened.

He couldn't stop thinking about Bay's words. He didn't see anything wrong with their situation, although he did admit it was awkward. How was Percy supposed to ignore that he was still a prisoner, though? This went beyond waking up with morning wood. Having to deal with that with one of his jailers made him uncomfortable. Or maybe it was Bay who made him uncomfortable. If he thought about it, he had to admit that he didn't view Bay as a jailer. They weren't friends, but they were mostly friendly, and Percy clung to that. Maybe if he tried being Bay's friend, it would be easier for him to relax.

Could they be friends? Bay was a fallen hero, and he was trying to convince Percy to change sides and abandon the conclave. Percy was resisting, but he couldn't deny that the conversations he'd had with Bay and the stories he'd heard at dinner yesterday had taken a chunk out of his certainty and the respect he had for the conclave. He wasn't quite ready to abandon them yet, and he would never admit it to anyone, but he'd finally allowed himself to think about the conclave and what they did, and he didn't like it.

He didn't *want* to think about it right now. He didn't know what the day would be like, but even though he was out of his cell, he was still a prisoner. What would that mean? He'd have to follow Bay during the day, but he doubted the fallen heroes would allow him to sit on his ass and do nothing. Maybe they'd planned something for him, or maybe Bay would find something for him to do.

Whatever the case, as long as they never talked about morning wood again, Percy would be happy.

Bay was still thinking about the way he and Percy had woken up by the time they walked into the kitchen. Breakfast wasn't as serious as dinner, and the fallen heroes didn't usually eat it together. Most of them liked to sleep in unless they were going on a mission, which Bay understood. He wouldn't be awake at this hour of the morning if Percy hadn't woken him up by freaking out.

It was still strange to be able to feel what happened to Percy's body. Bay was thankful that what he could feel was limited to that and didn't include Percy's emotions, because he didn't think he'd be able to live through that. Percy was a bundle of anger, fear, confusion, and embarrassment. Bay had no doubt Percy was feeling other emotions, especially when it came to his siren half. They hadn't talked about it yet, but he wanted to.

He still didn't understand how Percy had hidden his siren half from the conclave for all this time. He wanted to ask, but first, he had to figure out what he and Percy were supposed to do today.

He stuffed a piece of bacon into his mouth and chewed as he thought. He and Percy couldn't leave the house. Bay couldn't allow Percy to understand where it was, even though it was warded and hidden. Thanks to Cecil, the conclave would never be able to find them using spells. They probably wouldn't even try, since they didn't have that kind of magic. They'd have to ask a mage to help, and they'd never do that.

But showing Percy where the house was located was out. They could walk around in the forest, which would probably make Percy happy, considering he'd been locked up for a month, but they had to stay on the property. They also had to make sure Percy didn't see or hear anything sensitive. That would be even harder, considering Bay was one of Mordred's seconds. For now, they should probably agree that Eudocia should take care of everything Percy shouldn't hear.

She wouldn't be happy about that.

But it would be worth it. Bay glanced at Percy, who was

eating breakfast next to him at the kitchen island. He looked more relaxed, and he was even talking to Isaac. He seemed to have an easy enough time ignoring Tryg's glare, which Bay found funny. A lot of fallen heroes didn't like Tryg, not because of what he was, but because of how he behaved when it came to the man he loved. Bay knew something of Isaac's background, so he understood. He also liked that even though Tryg was present every step of the way, making sure no one hurt Isaac, he still wasn't stopping Isaac from making friends and talking to people. He was there if Isaac needed him, but otherwise, he didn't intervene.

Percy was more comfortable with Isaac than with anyone else so far, which probably made sense, since Isaac was human. Percy hadn't been merely human in a long time, but he still clung to the knowledge that he was supposed to protect humanity. He might not have realized Isaac was immortal, so that could change once he did, but even though Isaac would never die unless he was killed, he was still entirely human.

"I just don't understand why you can't consider it," Isaac was saying.

They were talking about the conclave, which was why Bay was surprised Percy hadn't clammed up. Usually, when Bay brought up the subject, Percy went ramrod straight and became so tense he might break if Bay touched him. Isaac was getting a different reaction, which made Bay curious.

"I can consider it," Percy said. "And I'll be the first to admit the conclave isn't perfect. But they've been in charge for thousands of years. Protecting humans was what they were created for, and they're doing their best."

"I don't believe that. I think they're hiding behind their mission of protecting humans and using it as an excuse to kill supernatural creatures."

"They kill supernatural creatures only because they're dangerous."

"I agree that some are, but most don't want anything to do with humans." Isaac sat up straighter. "And remember that the man I love is one of those creatures you're talking about. Should I be afraid you'll try to kill him just because of what he is?"

Percy's focus finally jumped to Tryg. Tryg grinned, but there was nothing happy about the gesture. Instead, it made him look even creepier than he already looked hovering over Isaac, and Percy quickly looked away.

"He's killed people," Percy said, ignoring Tryg.

"He has. It doesn't make him a bad person. Besides, I don't think the conclave can decide who should or shouldn't die. And what about humans who don't deserve to live?"

Percy shook his head. "The conclave doesn't decide that."

"But they do decide which supernatural creature needs to die. How does that make sense? If they truly want to protect humans, they should protect us against anything that could hurt us, including other humans."

Percy looked like his head was about to explode, so Bay thought it was time to end this. He stuffed the last bite of toast into his mouth, then got to his feet. "Are you almost done?" he asked Percy.

Percy blinked, then looked down at his plate as if surprised to realize he was still eating breakfast. "Almost. Do we need to go?"

"As soon as you're ready."

It only took a few minutes for Percy to finish eating his breakfast. He rinsed his plate and placed it into the dishwasher, then turned to look at Bay. Bay waved at Isaac, nodded at Tryg, and led Percy out of the room. Percy hadn't seen much of the house yesterday, so the first thing on Bay's list was to show him around.

He decided to start in the entrance. "As you probably realized by now, most fallen heroes live here in this house. Some live in towns close by, but they come anytime we need them. There's a special area beyond the house where we can create portals."

"The property is warded," Percy said.

It wasn't a question, and Bay wasn't surprised he knew. It would make sense to ward the house where the fallen heroes lived.

"It is. Cecil takes care of it now, but he's not the only mage who put his hands on the wards." This way, Percy would know it wouldn't be easy to break them, not even for the conclave.

They walked through the house as Bay pointed things out.

"As you can see, the house is surrounded by forest on three sides and faces the lake on the fourth. If you want to go down to the lake to swim or anything like that, just let me know. There's also a pool, and it's closer to the house. Going down to the lake is a bit of a trek."

The house sat back from the lake's rocky shore. Going down involved a lot of stairs, and the pool was more accessible. Still, sometimes, nothing beat a swim in the lake.

"I don't think I'll be doing a lot of swimming," Percy drawled.

Bay nodded. In the end, Percy was still a prisoner, even though he was free of his cell.

"There's plenty to do in the house," Bay continued. "The playroom has a bar and a pool table, and of course, there's the theater room. There's also a library, and you're welcome to use any of these."

"You do realize that to use one of those rooms, you'd have to come with me, right?"

Bay nodded. "I know, and I'm sorry about that. There's no way out of it."

Percy looked like he wanted to protest, but in the end, he just shook his head. "So basically, I'm welcome to use most of the house, but I can't because of you. That sounds great."

Bay winked. "Or we could do all those things together. I can be fun when I want to be." And when he was with the right person, which he suspected Percy might be. "Come on. Let me show you the room we use for meetings and the offices."

Showing him those things might be the wrong thing to do, but Bay wanted Percy to know he trusted him. He didn't entirely yet, but if Bay didn't give Percy anything, what incentive would Percy have to join the fallen heroes?

Percy wasn't surprised at how big the house was. He *was* surprised that Bay had shown him where the offices were, but then, it wasn't like he could go around poking his nose in, since he was stuck with Bay.

"Now, the chores."

That got Percy's attention. "How does it work with so many people living here?" He didn't think it worked like with the conclave. The conclave members themselves never did anything. The younger heroes still in training had to take care of that. They did laundry, cooked, and cleaned for the entire conclave and the working heroes. Percy had done that when he'd still been training. He'd hated it, but once he'd become a full-fledged hero, he hadn't seen a problem with it anymore. Maybe he should have. Now that Bay explained how it worked here, it didn't feel right to make the younger heroes do everything.

"Everyone is expected to help," Bay said. "That will include you, although of course, we'll make sure you can actually do whatever you need to do, considering the situation. We take turns cooking and cleaning the areas where we spend most of our free time. The playroom can become a bit messy, especially after a party. And of course, everyone cleans their own rooms."

"I'll do whatever you need me to do," Percy told him.

That seemed to surprise Bay, who blinked. "Really? Because I remember how it works with the conclave, and it's not like this."

"So? I'm an adult. I can clean up after myself." And after a few fallen heroes.

Bay stared for a moment before nodding. "Good. Do you have any questions?"

"Not at the moment." Not about the house, anyway. But Percy was curious about Bay and his family. He hadn't been able to stop thinking about it since Bay had told him.

It made him miss his father even more than he already did. When he thought about everything Bay had, he couldn't help but hate the conclave for taking his father from him. He'd never get him back. He'd been the only one to accept Percy's siren half and not hate him for it or try to kill him. He hadn't known what to do with it, but he hadn't tried to make Percy feel bad about it.

What would it feel like to have what Bay had? It wasn't just Bay's human family Percy was thinking about, either. He'd seen Bay with the fallen heroes, including Mordred. They were his family, and nothing like the heroes who worked with the conclave were.

Percy and the others had never been allowed to make friends or become close. The fallen heroes had, and it showed in every interaction they shared. Percy could become a part of it if he joined the fallen heroes.

But that would mean leaving everything behind. It wouldn't be the first time he'd done it. He'd left everything behind when the conclave had taken him away from his father. This wouldn't be the same, though. What would Percy do if he left the conclave?

He wouldn't have to obey their orders anymore, including

not having relationships and not becoming friends with other heroes. He'd never thought much about it, but now that he did, he wanted someone to love and who would love him. Joining the fallen heroes would be the only way for him to have that.

He'd never get his father back, but he could have a family. The fallen heroes could become that for him, and Percy found he wanted that. He was cautious about all of them, and he didn't trust them, but that would change in time. Besides, he didn't have to trust them to like them.

Could Percy really be considering doing this? It felt like a betrayal, but the more he thought about what the conclave had taken away from him, the more he wanted to leave them behind and say fuck it. He wanted to have breakfast with Isaac and talk to him about the human world and how Isaac viewed the supernatural one. He wanted to find out more about Cecil's powers.

He wanted to spend more time with Bay.

"Percy? Are you okay?" Bay suddenly asked.

Percy blinked. He hadn't realized it, but they'd stopped walking, and Bay was worried because Percy wasn't answering any of the questions he'd no doubt asked.

"I'm fine," Percy said, but he knew he didn't sound fine.

He looked around. He'd never seen this room, but it had to be the library. The floor was the same dark wood as in the rest of the house, but like everywhere else, a carpet blocked most of it from sight. On the left was a big fireplace, while the walls on the right were covered with shelves heavy with books. Right in front of Percy, the wall of big windows opened on the lake. A couch invited readers to sit, get lost in books, or maybe take a nap. There was also a desk and a few chairs, and they felt safer to sit in with Bay, so Percy moved toward them.

He didn't sit behind the desk but rather in front of it. He looked at the shelves, trying to find books he'd read. He didn't have much time to read or do anything else, not when the conclave sent him on missions almost every day.

"You're worrying me," Bay said as he sat in the chair next to Percy's.

Percy licked his lips. "I'm sorry. I was thinking."

"Do you want to talk about it?"

Percy shook his head, then nodded. He didn't know what he wanted. "You and the other heroes are very close, aren't you?" he asked instead.

Bay didn't look surprised at the question. "We are. Especially the ones who live here. You can't share a house and not be close, I guess, even when the house is as big as this one."

"You have the same kind of relationship with your family?"

"No. I don't see them nearly as often," Bay said as he leaned back in his chair. "They know there's something strange about me. The older ones know I'm not aging, and I guess it freaks them out a bit. Most are very accepting of what I am, though."

"You told them?"

"No. I never told them anything. They probably don't even know who I am exactly. But they've seen me around since they were children. I wish I could spend more time with them, and I do with some of the youngest members, but it's dangerous, both for them and for me. It would be too easy for my enemies to find my family and use them against me."

And by enemies, Bay meant the conclave.

The conclave was supposed to protect humans, but sometimes, they killed them instead, like the heroes' families. They wouldn't hesitate to eliminate Bay's family, and Percy found he was angry at the thought. He understood why Bay stayed away from them, but it wasn't fair.

"My father was human," he said. He hadn't intended on telling Bay about his parents, but Bay had opened up to him, and it made Percy feel like he should do the same. Bay hadn't asked today, and he wouldn't. But Percy wanted to tell someone about his father and what he'd done for him.

Bay nodded but didn't say anything, and it was easy for Percy to close his eyes and continue. "But my mother wasn't. I never knew her. My father didn't go into details about what had happened between them, but I know they met and fell in love. He lived by a lake, and apparently, that's where she lived. Inside the lake, I mean. She was a siren."

Percy could remember his father explaining all of this to him.

"So they met and fell in love, and she got pregnant. They couldn't get married because, well, she wasn't human. But they were happy together for a time. Then one day, she disappeared. I was only a baby then, and my father tried to find her, but he couldn't. There had been rumors about people going around asking questions about creatures, and he thinks they found her."

Bay made a strange sound. "You mean the conclave killed your mother?"

Percy blinked his eyes open. He'd never thought about that. Was the conclave responsible for what had happened to his mother? There was no way for him to know, not after three hundred years. "I don't know. My father never found out if she was dead or not. But he told me about her. He told me how beautiful she was, how much she loved me."

And Percy had lost them, and apparently, the conclave was responsible for both those losses.

Bay was surprised and ecstatic that Percy was talking about his family. *This* was what he'd wanted when he'd decided to get Percy out of the cell. He'd thought it would make it easier for Percy to see Bay and the others as people rather than enemies, and he'd been right. There was no way Percy would be telling Bay any of this if he didn't trust him. He'd even admitted he was half siren, for fuck's sake.

"So you grew up without your mother," Bay said softly.

"I did. My father did his best so I didn't miss anything, and he was great."

But then, Percy had lost him, too. Bay wanted to find the conclave and kill all of them for Percy's sake.

"He loved me, even though I wasn't fully human. He never wanted me to change, although it wasn't always easy for me to hide what I was. But he helped me there, too. Once he realized I had the same ability as my mother, he came up with a mix of herbs that suppressed that ability. I think my mother told him about it before she disappeared."

That explained how Percy had managed to hide what he was from the conclave. "That's why the conclave never realized what you were?" he asked.

Percy nodded. "I knew what those herbs were, so even after I was taken from my father, I continued taking them. These days, I take pills that have some of the same ingredients and effects."

"But since you've been here for a month, you weren't able to take your pills."

"And that's why my ability surfaced again." Percy hesitated. "You don't seem to have a problem with what I am."

"I don't."

"How can you not? I'm what the conclave warned us against. I'm a supernatural creature who can hide what he is. It would be easy for me to use my ability against you, yet you seem to trust I won't. How?"

Bay had thought about that. Percy could use his ability, but with the bracelets and the spell on them, what he could do was limited. Still, he could convince Bay to leave the house with him and never come back. He could take Bay straight to the conclave and let them take care of the spell between them.

Bay didn't think he would. He hoped he wasn't wrong.

"I'm trying to show you that there's an alternative life for heroes, one that doesn't include the conclave," he explained. "I can't say it's perfect, because it's not. With so many heroes living here, sometimes we fight. Sometimes, we don't want to go against the conclave. It's kind of terrifying. We don't want to kill heroes who still work for the conclave, but we have to when they attack us, and it's not a good feeling. No matter what you do, you're still our brothers, and if you don't realize what the conclave is doing, it makes sense for you to continue working for them. That's why we always try to talk to the heroes and convince them to see the conclave for what it truly is."

"And that's why you didn't kill me right away and kept me prisoner instead."

Percy didn't sound angry. If anything, he sounded like he finally understood what Bay had been telling him from the beginning. "Exactly. You're not the first hero we've done that to. Constantine was one of the most recent ones, for example."

Percy groaned. "Don't mention him, please."

"You sound like you don't like him."

"He's just a lot. I think he wants to be my friend, and he won't take no for an answer."

Bay grinned. "That sounds like Constantine, all right. But he's a good guy. You should give him a chance."

"Maybe I will."

If he stayed. Percy didn't have to say it.

"It's also why we reached out to the heroes through a video message," Bay continued. "We told them what we know the conclave has done over the years and what we believe they're trying to obtain through that. Not all heroes believed us, but some want out, and they reached out to us."

"You're going to help them?"

"We will. Even if they don't want to fight with us, we want them to be free to live their lives and stop obeying orders they don't agree with. There are a lot more fallen heroes than live in this house. Some work with us, but most don't. We keep in touch, just to make sure they're okay, but they live normal lives, or as normal as they can, considering they're immortal. A lot have found families and have fallen in love, some with supernatural creatures. Leaving the conclave would allow you to do that. It would give you the freedom to be who you want."

Bay hesitated. He knew how touchy this topic was for Percy, but Percy had been the one to bring it up, so Bay hoped he wouldn't freak out. "Hiding what you are can't have been easy, especially for close to three hundred years," he said.

"It actually was. With the pills, I was barely aware that I wasn't entirely human."

"But you still had to hide part of yourself."

"It was fairly easy to if I didn't think about it. I focused on the conclave's mission, on protecting humanity."

And now, Bay knew he'd learned that protecting humanity wasn't what the conclave truly wanted and that he'd been a weapon to obtain what they did want. "Do you think you'll be able to go back to hiding your siren half?"

Percy didn't answer right away, which Bay took as a good sign. He was thinking about it instead of replying automatically.

"It would be easy for me to do if I started taking the pills again," Percy said.

"It might be, but is it something you want to do? Or would you rather learn about your ability and how to use it to save people?" He would be an excellent addition to the fallen heroes. By working with supernatural creatures, the fallen heroes had an advantage over the conclave. Percy, especially, would have one because he'd been a hero for so many years.

"I don't know," was the only answer Percy gave.

Bay didn't mind. They'd taken a lot of steps forward today, steps he hadn't expected they would take. It was normal for Percy to need time to think about all of this and make a decision. Bay didn't need an answer today, so he settled in his chair and reached for one of the books on the shelves while Percy stared out the window.

They had chores to do and work, but it could wait. This was an important moment, and Bay wanted Percy to have all of it without worrying about anything else.

Percy truly didn't know. It was tempting to think he might be able to let his siren half through and work on accepting it, but could he leave the conclave behind?

It was getting more and more tempting to do just that. What had the conclave given Percy? They'd used him since they'd found him. They'd torn him away from his father and the only family he had. They'd kill him if they knew what he was. They'd made him do things he hated himself for.

He was a coward. Unlike Bay and the other fallen heroes, Percy hadn't been brave enough to leave. He'd continued obeying orders, even when he knew they were wrong. He'd buried his head in the sand and had told himself that the conclave knew what they were doing and that obeying their orders didn't make him a monster.

But it did. It wasn't his siren half that made him monstrous. It was what he'd done *willingly*.

He didn't think he could ever go back to the conclave and work for them again, and it had nothing to do with his siren half. The thought that if he left the conclave, he'd be able to accept himself was an incentive, though. He didn't know how he'd do it, but the first step could be talking to the supernatural creatures who lived with the fallen heroes.

Percy didn't know if they'd agree to talk to him. Cecil already had, but he'd been curious about the bracelets and the spell. He'd wanted to know if they worked, and the only way for him to find out was to talk to Percy and Bay. It didn't mean he wanted to do it again.

But what about Amyas? He'd seemed relaxed enough when he'd come to Percy's cell to talk to him about what he was. Besides, he knew sirens. Maybe he could help Percy accept what he was and learn how to control it. Right now, it was hard for Percy to use his ability to convince people to do what he wanted. If he managed to control it, he could help the fallen heroes against the conclave.

Was that something he could do? Could he go against the conclave and everything he'd believed in for three hundred years after only a month with the fallen heroes? He'd promised himself he wouldn't allow them to convince him that what he and the conclave were doing was wrong, but they had. There was no denying that, not anymore, not to himself.

He also had to think that Bay would be right there with him, whatever he decided. Unless Percy wanted to go back to the conclave, he was stuck with Bay, at least for now. He wouldn't be free from Bay unless he passed to the fallen heroes' side, and he suspected that even then, it would take a while for them to trust him. Bay was different, and Percy was relieved that at least one person wasn't considering killing him, but could he use Bay as a crutch?

Percy licked his lips and looked at Bay. He was still sitting in his chair, reading a book. He hadn't pushed and had instead given Percy time to think about things. Percy didn't understand why Bay had done any of this or why he'd decided to give him a chance, but now, he was grateful for it. He wanted to give something back.

He cleared his throat, getting Bay's attention. "Do you think it would be a problem if I talked to Amyas and the other supernatural creatures who live in the house?"

Bay closed his book and looked at Percy. "I suppose it depends what you want to talk to them about."

"I won't be rude or insult them." Although Percy could understand why Bay was hesitant. "But I can't deny what I am anymore. It might only be half of me, but it doesn't change that I'm a supernatural creature, or that I have no idea what to make of it. I don't know how to control my ability. If I could, I could help you. More importantly, I don't want it to get out of control when I don't need it."

Percy could too easily imagine what would happen if he used his ability on one of the fallen heroes or any other person who lived in the house. Even if it wasn't on purpose, he doubted anyone would give him the benefit of the doubt. Some would be happy to use it as an excuse to get rid of him.

"Does that mean you're ready to accept your siren half?" Bay asked.

"I think so. I can't make any promises, because I have no idea what will happen, but you're right. It's part of me, and even though it was easy to ignore, I shouldn't have to." Especially since the fallen heroes seemed to want Percy to be himself. It might just be Bay, but Percy didn't think so.

Bay grinned. "That's what I wanted to hear. And just so you know, no one here will care what you are."

Percy snorted. "Everyone cares that I'm a hero."

"They care that you work for the conclave, and what you are has nothing to do with that. You know we work with supernatural creatures, and you won't be any different."

"Except that you don't trust me."

"Not yet. But give us a reason to trust you, and we will. Once again, that has nothing to do with what you are. We've all been through it. All the heroes we managed to convince to come to our side have. You should talk to Constantine. He remembers well how it is after you leave that cell, and I'm sure he could give you pointers."

Percy groaned. "Do I have to?"

Bay grinned. "Not if you don't want to, but do you think you'll be able to avoid him much longer?"

Since Percy was stuck with Bay and Bay seemed intent on having Percy and Constantine talk, he didn't think so. Maybe he should give a thought about going back to his cell, after all.

CHAPTER EIGHT

Things were going well, much better than Bay had expected. A lot of that had to do with Percy and his willingness to give the fallen heroes a chance and accept his siren half. He still had doubts about the conclave and what they were doing, but it stemmed from having obeyed them for all these years. Bay could understand that. Even though he'd been away from the conclave for hundreds of years, he'd still worked for them for a long time. He'd obeyed their orders, even when he wasn't okay with them. He'd killed creatures who hadn't deserved it, and he still felt guilty about it. He could do nothing to change the past, and Percy would have to learn to deal with it, just like Bay and the other heroes had.

All of them had obeyed the conclave's orders, which meant that all of them had blood on their hands. It wasn't easy to accept, but Percy wasn't alone.

Bay rolled his head on the pillow to look at Percy, who was still sleeping. that was a minor miracle considering he tended to wake up before Bay most days. Bay suspected it had a lot to do with trying to hide his body's normal reactions, but they hadn't talked about that again, and Bay wouldn't bring it up if Percy didn't. The last thing he wanted was to embarrass Percy, and that *would* happen if he tried talking about it.

Percy was exhausted for a reason. Even though he was used to working in teams as a hero, it was very different from what was happening here. Now, he worked with Amyas and Cecil to get his ability under control, and it took a lot out of him. He also had to follow Bay around when Bay did his own job, and Bay understood why he was exhausted. He wasn't used to having so many people around who wanted to talk to him and get to know him. Most of the heroes in the house had started to relax around him. Everyone wanted to get to know him, and it was a lot.

Bay reached for his phone on the nightstand. Since Percy was sleeping so nicely, he didn't want to wake him up to go downstairs for breakfast before all the food in the fridge was gone. Maybe he could do something nice for Percy.

"Hello?" Amyas asked when he answered.

"I was wondering if you could do me a favor."

"I suppose it depends. What favor do you need?"

"Percy is exhausted, and he's still sleeping. Besides, you know he doesn't deal well with the chaos that happens during meals. I was wondering if you could bring up something to eat for both of us? Nothing elaborate. Even fruit and bread will be enough."

"That sounds like you're having breakfast in bed," Amyas said.

"I don't think we will. I just want Percy to be able to take a breather before he has to go back to the madness that is the house."

"I'll do it, but only because I like him."

Bay was surprised to hear that. "Do you? Because I know the two of you didn't have the best start."

"You mean because he tried to attack my village? Or because he was rude when I brought him and Mordred food when they were prisoners?"

Thankfully, Amyas's tone was teasing. "You're a better man than I am. I would have let him starve."

Amyas laughed. "If I had, I wouldn't be with Mordred now. But yes, I do like Percy. Now that I know him, I realize that even though he worked for the conclave, he didn't have a choice. None of you had one. You were taken from your families when you were children and brainwashed. It takes a strong person to see through that and realize that the only people you trust are evil."

Bay was touched. Sometimes, he wondered how the supernatural creatures who lived in the house could do it. He'd killed many of them, and they were aware of that. Still, they'd forgiven him and the other fallen heroes, and they'd made themselves at home. As far as Bay was concerned, they were the strong ones, not him.

It didn't take long for Amyas to be knocking on the door. Bay slid out of bed, trying not to wake up Percy, who was still sleeping. If Bay knew him, he'd be bothered that Bay had let him sleep so long. Bay didn't care. If Percy didn't take care of himself, Bay would do it for him.

Thankfully, the door was close enough to the bed that Bay could reach it without crossing their six foot limit. He opened it, already smiling and a *thank you* on his lips for Amyas, but that wasn't who Bay found on the other side of the door.

Bay blinked. "Aurelia?"

She smiled at him. "I haven't seen you in a while, so when Amyas said he was bringing you breakfast, I volunteered to come in his place," she said. Her long blonde hair was gathered in a ponytail, and her brown eyes gleamed with something Bay couldn't identify.

She was holding a tray with two plates of food on it. Amyas had gone all out, and instead of the fruit and bread Bay had expected, he'd piled the plates with eggs, bacon, and toast. There was also coffee, and Bay made a mental note to thank Amyas when he next saw him.

He reached for the tray, but Aurelia didn't let go. "You've been hiding with your hero," she said.

"I wasn't hiding. You know we're stuck together." Although Bay had to admit he didn't mind it.

Aurelia finally let go of the tray. She didn't step away and instead reached for Bay's face. She cupped one of his cheeks, running her thumb over his cheekbone.

Bay and Aurelia had been lovers once, and they sometimes still were. He supposed they were more friends with benefits, since there were no feelings between them except friendship. He realized he didn't miss her. He hadn't even thought about her, although he wasn't sure if that was because of the conclave and all the problems they created or because of Percy.

"You know where to find me when you're finally free of him," she purred.

Even though Bay had no intention of taking her up on that, he could feel his body react. It became worse when she slid her hand down from his cheek to his chest, then l lower. She'd never been shy, and today wasn't any different. She cupped Bay's cock, gently squeezing until she could feel it harden in her palm. Then, she let it go and took a step back, winking at him.

Bay swallowed. It had been a while since he'd had sex with anyone, but he usually didn't mind taking care of things by himself in the shower. That hadn't happened since he and Percy had been linked together, though. Bay hadn't wanted to make Percy uncomfortable.

At least Percy was still asleep.

Bay watched Aurelia walk away for a moment before shaking his head and taking a step back into the room. He closed the door behind himself and turned, expecting to see Percy still in bed, but he wasn't. The bathroom door was closed, but that wasn't what worried Bay.

If Percy was awake, he'd heard what Aurelia had said, and he'd felt what she'd done to Bay's body.

Bay groaned. Their next conversation wouldn't be easy or comfortable.

Percy's hands clutched the border of the sink. He stared at them and breathed, trying to get rid of the arousal that was tightening his groin.

He'd felt Bay get out of bed earlier at the knock on the door. He hadn't known what was happening, so he'd stayed in bed, at least until he'd felt *it*. Whoever was there—and from the voice, it was a woman—Bay wanted them.

Percy had run to the bathroom, not understanding why he felt so devastated. So what if Bay was attracted to someone? It was none of Percy's business. He and Bay weren't together, even though the bracelet meant they couldn't be apart. They weren't even friends, not really. Percy had to keep that in mind and remember that Bay had an entire life without Percy. He hadn't said anything about having a girlfriend, but Percy wouldn't be surprised if he did. It sure felt like it.

Percy took a deep breath, then another. He didn't care who Bay was with. He didn't care about the fact that Bay had an erection. What he did care about was that *he* had one, and he didn't want Bay to see it. It was bad enough that he had to feel what Bay felt. Hopefully, Bay didn't know what was happening to Percy's body, but since Percy couldn't be sure, he quickly stripped and stepped into the shower. He didn't wait for the water to warm—instead, he threw his body under the cold spray.

His entire body shuddered, and he fought the urge to step away. Even when the water warmed, he kept it as cold as he could stand it and spent as much time as possible under it. The problem was that he couldn't escape Bay. No matter how much he wanted to, Percy had no other option than to go back to the bedroom. It was already bad enough that Bay was no doubt standing just outside the door. Percy wasn't in pain, which meant they weren't too far apart.

He wanted to stay in the bathroom forever, but instead, he forced himself to turn the water off. He quickly dried off, then had to put his pajamas back on. He didn't mind, but he wished he had something better to cover himself. Jeans would have done the trick, but as it was, Bay would be able to see if Percy was hard.

Percy looked down. He wasn't at the moment, and he hoped that whatever had happened earlier was over.

There was a tentative knock on the door. "Percy? I don't want to rush you, but breakfast is here, and I need to use the bathroom," Bay said.

Percy nodded at himself and strode toward the door. He flung it open and, avoiding to look at Bay, stepped back into the bedroom. Bay hesitated, but in the end, he hurried inside and closed the door behind himself.

Since Percy couldn't go anywhere, he looked at the tray Bay had placed on the dresser. The smell of food made his stomach growl, and he grabbed a piece of bacon from one of the plates. He stuffed it into his mouth, staring at the wall in front of him, convincing himself he didn't care that Bay was attracted to someone who wasn't him.

When had he started to want Bay to be attracted to him, anyway? He was still a prisoner, and he had to keep that in mind. It didn't matter that Bay was a good person, that he'd listened to him, and that he was helping him to accept his siren half. For now, they were technically enemies. Maybe, if they were lucky, they'd become friends eventually, but Percy couldn't count on that, and he couldn't decide to stay because of it.

Bay came out of the bathroom, and Percy still avoided looking at him. Bay took the tray and headed toward the sitting area by the windows, and Percy could only follow him. They both settled into an armchair, and Bay gestured at the tray. "Take one of the plates. I had someone bring up breakfast."

Percy gritted his teeth. "I'm aware.".

There was a pause before Bay said, "I wanted to do something nice for you. I know you're overwhelmed with the number of heroes living in the house and wanting to talk to you, and I thought you could do with a quiet breakfast for once. But we can go downstairs if you'd rather be with the others."

Percy shook his head and took the plate from which he'd stolen the bacon. "This is fine."

They ate in silence. Percy could tell Bay wanted to ask what was going on, but he didn't, and that was fine with Percy. Percy was avoiding looking at Bay, not knowing what to do or even how to react. Who was the woman at the door? Bay wanted her, and he'd be happier if he wasn't stuck with Percy. Percy wanted to offer to go back to his cell, but there was no way he'd do that just so Bay could get laid. He was never going back in that cell. He'd had enough of it.

Percy hoped that once they were done eating, they'd dress and head downstairs. He placed his empty plate on the tray, got to his feet, then moved toward the dresser to grab some clothes. Everything would have been okay if Bay hadn't decided to follow him.

"What's going on?" he asked, cornering Percy by the dresser.

"Nothing. We have things to do, and we should start our day."

"You didn't say a word while we were eating. You look angry, and you showered."

"So what? I can't shower?"

Percy's tone was harsh, and Bay looked nonplussed. "Of course you can. But you didn't even take clean clothes with you in the bathroom. Something is going on, and I'd like to know what it is."

Percy shook his head and looked away. He couldn't afford to be vulnerable, especially not with Bay. He didn't want Bay to understand how conflicted and ashamed he was. He despised having to feel the same things Bay did, even if only physically. He didn't want to know when Bay was aroused or when Bay wanted to have sex with someone. He just wanted to be left alone and to get over whatever he was feeling. It wasn't love, but he couldn't deny he wanted Bay, and he hoped it was just because of the bracelets. It had to be. There was no way he'd want Bay in any other situation.

Since Bay was still crowding him, Percy tried to step away. Maybe he could hide in the bathroom again.

But before he could, Bay caught his wrist and pulled him back. "No," he said, his tone hard now instead of confused. "I want to know what's going on. Yesterday when we went to bed, you were okay. This morning, you act like you hate me again, and I don't want to go back to that. So tell me. What happened?"

Percy pulled on his wrist, but Bay didn't let go, and Percy had enough. He turned around, facing Bay and getting right in his face. "You know what happened! Did you do it on purpose? Did you do it because you knew how I would feel about it?"

Bay blinked and took a step backward, finally letting go of Percy. "What?"

"You should be ashamed of yourself. You know how uncomfortable I feel about those things, yet you allowed your girlfriend to—to make you feel that way. Is it because you wanted me to feel it? Because you wanted me to know about her? Couldn't you just tell me?"

Bay shook his head. "It's not what you're thinking."

"Of course it's not. It's never what I'm thinking, is it?"

Bay had turned away, but now he faced Percy. "Would you calm down? I didn't ask Aurelia to make me feel that way. I didn't want to make *you* feel that way, because I know how ashamed you are of it. You need to grow up, though. You're three hundred years old, yet you can't even say you have an erection. How fucked-up is that?"

"Not wanting to talk about sex doesn't make me a child." Percy was offended that Bay was even thinking it.

"Maybe not, but it makes you stuck up. When was the last time you had sex? Have you *ever* had sex?"

Percy spluttered. "Of course I have, but it's none of your business. It wouldn't be even if I hadn't."

"You're right. It wouldn't be. But what happened is a normal physiological reaction. You can't hold that against me, and you need to stop acting as if it's not normal."

Percy wasn't stuck up. Was it a crime not to want someone he barely knew to know he was aroused? Or not to want to know when Bay felt the same, especially for someone who wasn't Percy?

"I should go shower," Bay said.

But Percy wasn't done with him. He grabbed Bay's shirt before he could leave and pulled him closer. Their lips crushed together. It wasn't a good kiss. It was too hard, too harsh, and Bay hadn't been expecting it. When he didn't kiss back, Percy thought he'd made a mistake. He *knew* he'd made a mistake. He had no idea what he was doing, and he panicked. He started to move away, but then Bay kissed him back.

Bay had no idea what was happening, but he wasn't about to step away from it. Percy had initiated the kiss, and Bay would continue it.

He buried his hands in Percy's still too-long hair and held him close. The kiss was fierce, more a battle of their lips than anything else. It had none of the warmth Bay usually felt with lovers, but that didn't mean there wasn't affection in it.

There was. He didn't know when it had happened or if Percy felt the same way, but Bay liked Percy. More importantly, he was falling in love with him, and while he didn't know what it would mean or what would happen, he wouldn't hide from it. Even if this was the only time he and Percy did this, Bay would give it his all.

He'd give Percy all of himself.

Twisting, he slammed Percy's back against the wall. Percy made a strangled sound, but he didn't push Bay away, and he never stopped kissing him.

Percy was just a bit taller than Bay, not enough to be a bother as they kissed, but enough for Bay to be aware of it. He rose on his tiptoes, then glared at Percy when he felt him smile against his lips. Percy didn't say anything. He bit Bay's lower lip, then opened his legs to lower himself so they'd be at the same height. It gave Bay easier access, and it allowed them to be even closer to each other.

Bay slid a hand down Percy's chest, pausing to tweak a nipple through his shirt. Percy groaned and surged forward. Their teeth clicked together, but Bay ignored the slight pain. It was easy when his arms were full of Percy.

Bay cupped Percy's ass with one hand and used the other to push down Percy's pants. Percy was already hard, but then, so was Bay. Bay needed skin, but he didn't have the patience to rid Percy of his clothes, so he did the next best thing and grabbed Percy's cock.

Percy thrust his hips forward. His cock slid into Bay's hand, and Bay grinned, rubbing his thumb on the tip to spread the moisture. He tightened his hold and moved his hand up and down, enjoying the way Percy felt in his hand but even more, enjoying the power he had over him right now.

Maybe power wasn't the best word. If Percy wanted, he could push Bay away easily, and Bay felt better knowing that. But the fact that Percy *wasn't* pushing him away and was instead kissing him and sliding his hands under Bay's shirt to touch him made Bay feel like he was ten feet tall.

Percy's fingers caught in the waist of Bay's jeans. He struggled to undo them, and Bay wasn't any help since he was too busy both kissing Percy and jacking him off. He'd gotten his other hand in the back of Percy's pants and was cupping his ass, although his fingers slid ever so closer to Percy's hole every time Percy moved.

Percy hummed when he lowered Bay's pants. Since he'd done the hard work, Bay released him so he could grab both Percy's cock and his own in his hand. Percy seemed to like that idea, and he added his hand to the mix. The touch of smooth hardness against his cock made Bay cry out. How was it possible that he already felt so close to exploding? Was it because it had been so long since he'd had someone else's hand on him, or because he was doing this with Percy?

He didn't care, not at the moment.

Bay kissed Percy harder and dug his fingers into the soft flesh of Percy's ass cheek. He used that hold to keep Percy close as they undulated against each other. The head of Bay's cock rubbed against Percy's, reminding him why he enjoyed sex with guys so much. Percy's skin was smooth, but it stretched over hard muscle and a cock that made Bay want to weep, it felt so perfect against him.

Percy's body shuddered. Bay felt his cock twitch in his hand, then something warm hit his skin. He grinned and pushed his face against Percy's neck, biting him where everyone would be able to see it. He wanted the entire house to know what they'd done.

Then he came, too, and he couldn't think straight anymore. He couldn't think, period.

He buried his face against Percy's neck and inhaled his scent. He hadn't realized he wanted this with Percy, but now that they'd done it, he wanted to do it again and again.

Then Percy pushed him away.

Bay stumbled back, blinking as he tried to understand what was happening. Percy's cheeks were flushed, and his eyes were wide. He stared at Bay, still panting.

Bay reached for Percy, but Percy shook his head and slid sideways against the wall. He was already reaching for his pants to hike them higher on his hips. Bay took advantage of the distraction to kiss Percy on the cheek, but he didn't linger, even though he wanted to.

Percy looked like he didn't know what to do or say. He opened his mouth, closed it again, then asked, "Did you do it to convince me to stay?"

Bay laughed. He couldn't help it, even though Percy looked confused and angry. When Percy tried to move away, Bay shook his head and caught Percy's wrist, pulling him closer and kissing the inside of it, right where the bracelet linking them together sat.

"No, that's not why I did it."

"Why, then?"

"Because I wanted to. I don't know if you'll decide to stay and become a fallen hero, but I wouldn't do something like this to convince you. I'll be happy if you decide to stay with us, and more importantly, with me, but this has nothing to do with it."

Percy swallowed. "I don't understand."

Bay took a chance and kissed Percy's palm. "It's all right. I realize this came out of nowhere, and I can't say I'd thought about it before. But I like you, and yeah, I'm falling in love with you. I want to do this again, but you'll have to be the one to decide that."

And Bay hoped Percy wanted it as much as he did and that he hadn't just declared his love only to have Percy tell him he didn't feel the same way.

CHAPTER NINE

Bay was acting weird, and Percy wasn't sure what to do or even what had happened. He supposed it had to do with the fact that they'd had sex. It had happened a few days ago, and ever since, Bay had been strange.

He kept asking Percy if he was okay, and that wasn't all. If it was, Percy wouldn't have noticed. But Bay kept bringing him bottles of water, saving him the desserts he liked at dinner, and during movie night with the other fallen heroes, he'd made sure to pick a movie Percy enjoyed. Then he'd sat next to Percy and even wrapped his arm around Percy's shoulders. He hadn't seemed to care who noticed, and while Percy's cheeks had felt warm for the entire movie, he hadn't minded. Hell, he'd cuddled close to Bay, and he'd enjoyed himself.

What was going on?

Percy softly snorted to himself. Thankfully, Bay was talking with Thor as all of them ate lunch in the kitchen, so he didn't hear him. If he had, he'd no doubt have asked what was going on and if Percy needed anything.

Bay was acting strange, but then, so was Percy. Ever since they'd had sex, he wasn't quite sure how to behave. He knew what he wanted, but he wasn't used to anything like that, and he didn't know if Bay would welcome it. It was clear Bay didn't mind if the others in the house knew they were sleeping together, not given how touchy he'd been. He was always touching Percy in some way — an arm around Percy's shoulder, a hand on his knee, a kiss on the cheek. There was no hiding that they were having sex, and even though Percy was surprised at himself, he didn't mind.

But he wanted to know what was going on, dammit. He wanted to know what Bay was thinking.

Since he couldn't exactly ask, he decided to do the next best thing. He turned to Cecil, who was on the other side of him, talking to Isaac. When Percy cleared his throat, Cecil turned his attention to him and smiled.

"Did you need anything?" he asked.

Percy peered at Bay, but Bay was still talking with Thor. "I wanted to talk to you."

"I'm listening."

"I don't want Bay to hear."

Cecil frowned. "It has to do with him, then?"

"It does, but it's a good thing." Percy wrinkled his nose. "Or at least, I think so. That's why I have to talk to someone."

Cecil's eyes widened. "Oh, I see. Wait a second."

Percy obeyed. He didn't have a choice. He didn't know what kind of powers Cecil had or what he could do with them, but he hoped he had something that meant Bay wouldn't be able to hear their conversation.

Cecil muttered a few words, then grinned at Percy. "Go on."

Percy looked around. Everything still looked the same, and he had no idea what Cecil had done. "Bay won't be able to hear?"

"He won't. What's going on?"

Percy didn't know how to do this. He didn't have friends, or at least, he hadn't had friends until he'd arrived here. He didn't know if he'd consider Cecil a friend, but they were friendly enough that Percy wanted to talk to him. "Bay has been acting strange," he explained.

Cecil didn't look surprised. "Strange how?"

"He keeps bringing me things. Like earlier, when he got me that bowl of strawberries."

"He got it because they were the last ones, and he wanted you to have them."

"Why is he doing that, though? I don't understand."

Cecil stared at Percy for a second before shaking his head. "You truly don't, do you?"

"That's what I just said."

"Don't get offended. I just think it's sad that you can't even see how much Bay likes you. It's right in front of you, and he's not shy about it. He *wants* you to know he likes you."

Percy didn't have to ask what Cecil intended by *like*. It was obvious, even to him. "But why?"

Now, Cecil looked amused. "Why does anyone like anyone?"

"I work for the conclave. I'm his enemy. He should hate me, so why doesn't he? And why isn't he wary of my siren half?" Even Percy didn't like his siren, and he had to live with it. He knew that eventually he'd get used to being one, but it was still odd for him to think about it for now. He couldn't understand why Bay didn't have a problem with it.

Cecil's expression softened. "The fact that you're part siren doesn't mean you're bad. In the end, we're just humans with a quirk, aren't we?"

Percy snorted, louder this time. "That's a nice way to put it."

"I suppose it's easier for me to think of myself that way since I look human. You do, too. Why can't it be what you are? Your father was human."

Percy was still surprised at how easily he'd been able to talk to Cecil about his father. It seemed like now that he'd opened those doors, he couldn't close them again, and he didn't want to. Even though he'd never get his father back, he still wanted him in his life, and the best way to do that was to talk about him.

"The fact that we're not entirely human isn't a bad thing,

and you shouldn't be afraid of yourself or of whoever is different," Cecil continued.

"I'm not afraid."

"Are you sure? Isn't fear the reason you'd rather go back to the conclave than try to live your life as a half siren? Knowing what you know now, do you think you could stand up to the conclave?"

Percy didn't know how to answer. He wanted to say yes, but he wouldn't stand a chance if he fought the conclave. Right now, the conclave had the power, and no one was doing anything about it. The fallen heroes were trying, but there weren't enough of them. If they wanted to get rid of the conclave, they'd need more people.

Would Percy be one of those people? Even if he decided to be, it still wouldn't be enough. He was only one man and half siren. What could he do against the entire conclave? They were old heroes with a lot of experience and training. They would squash him like a bug, and they wouldn't give him a second thought.

That was one of the reasons Percy had decided not to go back. The conclave wouldn't hesitate to kill him if they knew what was happening, or that he was a half siren. It wasn't fair. He'd worked for them for close to three hundred years, yet he still didn't mean anything to them.

He could see the truth now. More importantly, he could accept it.

He meant something for the fallen heroes, or at the very least, for Bay. That was important. Percy had already made his decision, but it didn't feel like enough. Now that he'd seen and accepted how cruel the conclave was, he understood the fallen heroes' mission, and he wanted to help. He wanted to give them something useful they could use against the conclave, but what? How could the fallen heroes, no matter how many there were, take the conclave down?

Even though more fallen heroes were arriving every day at the house, it wouldn't be enough. What they needed was the help of supernatural creatures, and Percy felt like a traitor for even thinking it. Now that he had, though, he couldn't stop.

That was how the fallen heroes would win. They needed support, and the only place they could find it was in the supernatural community.

Percy was startled when Cecil patted his knee. He looked at the mage, wondering what he'd missed. Cecil just smiled at him. "I can see you're thinking, and I'm not sure if I told you what you wanted to hear, but when it comes to Bay, give him a chance. I know it has to be confusing for you, but he truly likes you. It's written all over his face when he looks at you."

Percy glanced sideways, and sure enough, Bay was looking at him. It made Percy's heart race, and he found himself smiling. Bay smiled back, and Percy wanted to believe Cecil. He wanted Bay to like him, and he wanted to stay here with him.

Bay couldn't help but peek at Percy as they walked away from the kitchen. Percy and Cecil had been talking, but Bay didn't know what about, which meant Cecil had used his magic. There was no way Bay wouldn't have heard the conversation otherwise, since he'd been sitting next to Percy. Bay wanted to ask, but if Percy wished for him to know, he'd tell him. He'd always been private, and that hadn't changed just because they were sleeping together.

"What do we have planned today?" Percy asked.

Bay grinned. "A vacation."

Percy looked confused. "What do you mean?"

Bay pressed a hand over his heart. "I should have known he didn't know what a vacation is," he said dramatically. "Don't worry. I'll show you."

Percy rolled his eyes. "I know what a vacation is. I just don't understand what you mean. We can't leave the house."

The bracelets and the spell still linked them, and for now, Bay had no intention of taking his off. That didn't sit well with him because it made him feel like he was forcing Percy to be with him, but it was too soon. Even though it seemed Percy had decided to stay with them, they needed more time — which made Bay feel strange because of how his and Percy's relationship had been evolving, and they had to talk about it, but not today.

Today, he had plans.

Bay hoped that whatever conversation Percy and Cecil had been having had gone well and meant that Percy was thinking about staying long-term. He didn't have to, even if he decided to stop working for the conclave. Bay didn't know what he and Percy were doing, but he wanted it to continue.

He guided Percy downstairs until they reached the pool. They could see it through the windows, and Percy's eyes were wide when Bay looked at him.

Bay gestured at the pool, grinning. "Welcome to your vacation."

"You brought me to the pool?"

"I told you there was one, but you haven't yet had time to explore it. I thought it would be a good idea."

"Thank you."

"There are swimming suits in those drawers." Bay pointed at a piece of furniture against the wall. The pool was outside, but the area inside was just as nice. There was a couch, armchairs, and a coffee table. There was also the bar, and during the summer, everyone spent a lot of time here. Bay and Percy were lucky to find it empty, although he supposed it was getting colder. Hopefully, Percy would still want to take a swim.

Percy grinned and opened the first drawer. He dug through the swimming suits, and Bay couldn't help but stare at him. He'd thought Percy would be happy, but not this much. For the first time since they'd met, Percy seemed to be excited about something, and Bay hoped that was a good sign.

Percy was the first in the water. He threw himself in it, his blond hair flying behind him. Bay watched as Percy sank to the bottom of the pool, then pushed himself up and started swimming back and forth. Bay couldn't stop smiling, and he could see Percy couldn't, either.

Percy had seemed interested in the pool when Bay had mentioned it during their tour of the house. Bay didn't know if Percy enjoyed it so much because he was half siren or just because he wanted a swim, but it didn't matter. As long as Percy was happy, Bay was, too.

He jumped into the water, far enough away from Percy so they wouldn't hit each other. He didn't fancy swimming, so instead, he stayed close to the edge of the pool, happy to watch Percy.

It took a while for Percy to stop swimming and come to Bay. When he did, he was grinning from ear to ear. Bay opened his mouth to ask if he was enjoying himself, but before he could, Percy kissed him.

Percy's skin was slick and cool, but Bay didn't hesitate to wrap his arms around him and pull him closer. They kissed until they were both out of breath and hard in their swimming suits.

"I take it you like this idea?" Bay asked.

Percy's smile was blinding. "I love it. Thank you."

"You don't have to thank me."

"I do. I'm not blind, Bay. I see how you take care of me every day. You always do nice things, and while I'm not sure I understand why you do them, I don't think it matters. I'm just grateful you're doing them."

"I do them because I care about you."

"Not because you want to convince me to stay?"

"Are we having this conversation again? Yes, I do want you to stay, but I doubt that allowing you to swim in the pool is the one thing that'll convince you."

"Probably not, but it's still nice," Percy murmured.

It was. They spent the afternoon alone at the pool. Bay didn't know if everyone was giving them a chance to be together or no one was interested in the pool today, but he didn't care. He had what he wanted, which was more time with Percy.

They kissed for a long time, then Percy went back to swimming. After that, he alternated, always coming back to Bay. They played in the water until the sun started to set and Bay's stomach growled.

"We should probably head inside for dinner," Percy murmured.

"There's some food here," Bay explained as he got out of the water and headed into the house. "It's only snacks, but it'll tide you over until dinner."

Percy bit his lower lip. "Do we really have to go to dinner?"

Bay hadn't expected that, but he shook his head. "We can stay here if you want."

Percy looked straight at him. "I don't want to stay here."

He moved forward, right into Bay's arms. They kissed, and Bay could feel the heat building. Once again, they were both hard, and Bay hoped Percy wouldn't shy away from it. Since they'd first had sex, he'd gotten better, but sometimes, he was still bashful about normal body reactions.

"I want to go back to our room," Percy murmured.

Bay was pretty sure his heart expanded two sizes. Percy had called the bedroom they shared *their* room, and Bay hoped it meant what he thought. "Then let's go back," he murmured back.

They cleaned up the pool area before heading back inside,

still wearing just their swimming suits. Bay could hear noise coming from the dining room, so dinner had started. He and Percy didn't stop, though. They could eat later, once whatever Percy wanted to do was over.

They stumbled down the hallways, laughing and holding hands. Bay was glad everyone was downstairs—he knew Percy didn't trust them enough to be this vulnerable in front of them yet. He trusted Bay, though, and Bay cherished that.

He always would.

It took him two tries to manage to open his bedroom door. Or was it their bedroom now? Bay had never been too touchy about his personal space or belongings, and he liked that Percy's presence was everywhere in his space now.

Bay was messy, while Percy was kind of a neat freak. Bay had been making an effort to pick up his dirty socks, although he didn't mind listening to Percy bitch at him and calling him a slob. There was always affection in his words, and Bay yearned for it.

He yearned for Percy.

Percy slammed the door behind them and was on Bay right away. They were both only wearing their swimming suits and a towel, but those quickly disappeared. Percy would complain they'd left damp spots on the carpet, but that was a problem Bay would deal with later. Hopefully, Percy would be well-fucked and not in any condition to think about the carpet.

They tumbled onto the bed. Percy's skin was damp and cold against Bay's, but it quickly warmed with the friction of their bodies rubbing together and the shared body heat. They rolled until Bay was under Percy, being kissed to within an inch of his life and yet, wanting more.

He slapped his hand on the mattress in the direction of his nightstand. "Lube," he groaned when Percy bit one of his collarbones.

Percy's head jerked up. "What?"

"Lube. It's in the drawer." So far, they hadn't done anything that required it, but Bay had every intention of finishing the day with Percy's cock in his ass.

Percy's swallowed, his Adam's apple bobbing. "Are you sure?"

"I wouldn't be offering if I weren't." Bay raised himself on one elbow and kissed Percy's lips. "But we don't have to do it if you don't want to." Bay and the others had already pushed Percy a lot. He didn't want to do that in a private setting, too.

Percy licked his lips and moved away from Bay and toward the nightstand. Bay flopped onto his back and wrapped a hand around his cock, pulling on it as he watched Percy open the drawer. Percy's eyes were wide as he turned again and he took in what Bay was doing.

Bay grinned and opened his legs. He trailed his fingers down from his cock to his hole. He might not have the lube, but that didn't mean he couldn't have a little fun and hopefully entice Percy to come closer instead of continuing to stare at him.

Bay pushed one finger into his body. It didn't feel the best, but he didn't have to wait long for Percy to start moving again. He fumbled with the lube, dropped it to the mattress, then snatched it again and opened it. Bay couldn't stop smiling. He might not know what their future would be like or even if they'd be together, but he was going to enjoy every second of what was happening.

Percy looked glorious naked, especially when his pale skin was flushed with arousal and his hair was all over the place. He looked nothing like the hard hero he'd been the first few weeks after Bay had dragged him here. He'd softened gradually, but never as much as he had since their first kiss, and Bay hoped it meant something. He wanted it to mean everything.

Percy knee-walked until he was between Bay's spread legs.

His hand shook when he reached for Bay's ass, and it told Bay everything he wanted to know. Percy wanted him. They'd talk about what it meant later, once Percy's life was less frantic and he had time to make decisions.

Percy's fingertip touched Bay's ass cheek, then his finger, and finally, his hole. He pulled his own finger out, groaning when Percy's replaced it. It felt good, better than when he did this to himself.

Bay hooked a leg around Percy's waist. He didn't need much prep, but he could tell this moment was heavy with meaning for Percy, so he let him do it at his own pace, even though he was pretty sure glaciers moved faster than Percy was. But the stretching was delicious, and Percy kept kissing what he could reach of Bay's body — his knees, the inside of his thighs, his ankles. Bay had never felt so cherished. Usually he was the one who took care of lovers. Now, Percy was taking care of him.

When he was finally ready, Percy removed his fingers from Bay's body and stretched over him. Bay wrapped his arms around him. This was sex, but not merely sex. Every move they made felt heavy with meaning, and he wanted Percy to know he could feel it, too.

They looked each other in the eyes as Percy entered Bay. Bay couldn't have looked away even if he'd wanted to. It didn't last long, because once Percy started moving, Bay couldn't focus on anything that wasn't the feeling of him inside his body and the way his hips snapped back and forth.

Bay clutched Percy's shoulders and held him close, pressing panting open-mouthed kisses to his lips, his jaw, and his cheeks. Percy shuddered, and his rhythm faltered. Bay knew he'd have to take care of himself, and that was more than okay with him. He let go of one of Percy's shoulders and grabbed his cock. The pressure and friction made him moan. The hair on Percy's stomach rubbed against the head of Bay's cock, and with the added movement of Bay's hand, he came before Percy.

That didn't stop Percy, who continued driving into Bay until he cried out. Bay could feel Percy's cock pulse inside his body, and he gently tightened his muscles, milking him until he slumped. Bay didn't let him go. He wrapped his arms around him, holding him close and hoping he'd never have to let go.

He wasn't sure he'd be able to if he had to.

Percy tried to catch his breath, but it wasn't easy when he was still plastered against Bay. He could feel every breath Bay took, every movement he made, and he wanted more. He wanted to feel Bay forever, and it scared him.

Percy rolled to the side. Bay reached for him instantly, hooking an arm around his waist so he couldn't go too far. He didn't say anything, but he didn't have to.

Being so close to Bay, thinking about the man he was and the others in the house, Percy couldn't avoid thinking about his past and what would be his future if he decided to go back to the conclave. Bay and the others assumed he'd decided to stay, but he hadn't yet made a conscious choice. He hadn't wanted to face what he'd done in the past and what the conclave had done to him.

He had to. Now probably wasn't the best moment to think about it, although maybe it was. Percy was safe, in Bay's arms, and he could hear the sound of people in the house. Even though he wasn't one of them yet, he knew they'd stand up to the conclave for him. That was more than he could say for any hero who still worked for the conclave.

Percy didn't want to go back. The conclave would kill him if they found out about his siren half, and now that he'd allowed himself to think about his parents, he couldn't forget again. He couldn't ignore what he was, what his mother had been, or that the conclave was responsible for him losing both his parents. He couldn't be sure when it came to his mother, but even if the conclave hadn't killed her, they would have if they'd found her. That was enough to make Percy never want to go back.

But did he have a place with the fallen heroes? Or with Bay? That was a question he didn't have an answer to. He remembered what Bay had said about some of the fallen heroes not working with them. They left the conclave, disappeared, and build themselves a life. Percy could do that, but he didn't want to. He wanted to stay with Bay and the fallen heroes and to help them destroy the conclave.

He needed answers. He'd already made his decision, but he wanted to know what was next.

When he looked at Bay, Bay was looking at him. His gaze was soft, and it hurt to think Percy might lose this, so he looked away.

"If I decide to leave the conclave, is there a place for me here?" he asked, his voice barely more than a whisper.

Bay settled closer. "There will always be a place for you here, no matter what happens."

"Even if we're not together?"

Bay propped himself up on his elbow and looked down at Percy. He cupped one of Percy's cheeks and gently kissed his nose. "Always," he said. "You'll *always* have a place here, even if you refuse to fight with us against the conclave, even if the two of us break up. We don't abandon people. As long as you don't work for the conclave anymore, you're one of us, which means we'll take care of you."

Percy's eyes burned. "It sounds unreal."

"I know. But Mordred has worked hard to make it happen. He wants heroes to be free, both from the conclave and to do what they want with their lives."

"But we won't be truly free from the conclave until we disband it."

Bay nodded. "That's true. We'll need more people to make that happen, and I hope you'll fight with us. The conclave is losing many heroes after the video Mordred sent, and from what we've been able to find out, they're reacting by being even more cruel. I'm glad you decided to stay, because I don't want you to go back to them, not knowing what they might do. I won't deny that we could use your help, but no one here is going to force you to do anything. We all understand how you feel. We've all been through it before. You only just now left the conclave, and we don't expect you to fight against them."

But Percy wanted to. He was angry at what the conclave had done to him, and he wanted revenge for what they'd taken from him. He wasn't surprised the conclave was being even crueler than before. It was how they worked. When they didn't get what they wanted, they obtained it through violence, and they had to be pissed over what Mordred had done. They wouldn't stop at anything to get to him, and even though Percy still wasn't sure he could trust Mordred, especially after the way they'd met and he'd kidnapped Percy, he wouldn't allow the conclave to hurt anyone Bay cared about.

What had happened to him? He'd never cared for anyone the way he cared about Bay, and he didn't know what to do with any of this. Were he and Bay a couple? Or were they just having sex? Was Percy convenient because the two of them were stuck together and it would be awkward for Bay to have sex with someone else, maybe the woman who had brought breakfast the other day?

Bay kissed Percy again, then lowered his body to the mattress. Percy rolled to his side so they could look at each other. He didn't have answers to those questions, and he was afraid to ask. Maybe it was better for him to focus on the conclave and what he could do to help instead. "I don't know if I can face the conclave," he said.

Bay nodded. He didn't look surprised or angry, which was a relief. "Then you won't have to."

"I'm not done talking."

Bay grinned. "All right. What else did you want to say?"

"I don't know if I can face the conclave or the other heroes," he repeated. "Thinking about fighting them makes me feel like a traitor. I know stepping away from the conclave was the right thing to do, but I still betrayed them. It doesn't mean I won't help. I might not be able to look them in the eyes, but I'll tell you everything I know about the conclave and the building, and I'll do anything you need me to do."

Percy would never get his family back, but he could have a new one. He hadn't allowed himself to think that until now, but he couldn't avoid it anymore. He wanted a family. He wanted what Bay and the fallen heroes were offering. If he decided to stay with them, he'd never be alone again, even if he and Bay didn't work out.

But Percy wanted them to work out. He'd never been in a relationship and had no idea what he was doing, but he thought Bay didn't mind. Maybe they could learn how to be together as a couple instead of Percy doing all this on his own. Whatever happened, though, there was one thing he was sure of.

The conclave was wrong when they ordered heroes to kill supernatural creatures just because of what they were. Percy should have realized that a long time ago, and he suspected he'd blame himself for that for a long time. If there was one chance for him to redeem himself, he'd take it. He might not be ready to face the conclave, but it didn't mean that if he had to, he wouldn't.

"As long as you're safe and happy, that's enough for me," Bay murmured. "But if you're ready to fight by our side, I welcome it. Together, we'll defeat the conclave."

And for the first time, Percy truly believed they would.

CHAPTER TEN

"We could use that entrance," Percy said, pointing at a spot on the blueprint.

Mordred tilted his head. "That wasn't there when I worked for the conclave."

"They added it a few decades ago, but not many heroes know about it. The only reason I do is that one of the conclave members asked me to use that entrance once when they needed to talk to me."

Mordred's eyes narrowed. "They didn't want anyone else to know about it."

Bay looked from one to the other. He almost couldn't believe what was happening. They were in Mordred's office, going over maps and blueprints to find a way to enter the building where the conclave was based. Mordred knew the place, since he'd been there many times when he was a hero, but it had changed a lot in the meantime. It had been several hundred years, after all. That was why he'd asked Percy if he could give a hand by pointing out what might have changed, and to everyone's surprise, Percy had agreed.

Bay had gone with him because, well, he and Percy couldn't be apart, but also because he didn't *want* to be away from Percy. The two of them were working things out much better than Bay had expected, and that was good to see. Soon they'd be able to get the bracelets off, and Percy would be allowed to move around on his own.

Bay was happy about that, but also sad. Having Percy around the house on his own meant that the fallen heroes trusted him, and Bay wanted that for him. Percy had been opening up more and more as the days passed, and while he wasn't quite part of their group yet, he would be. Bay could see it in the way Percy behaved with the fallen heroes and the way they viewed him. For Mordred to ask him to help with this, it meant he was trusted.

And Bay was happy about that. Percy wanted to do more and be useful, and the situation was giving him a chance to do just that. It was showing him that he had a place here with the fallen heroes, which was all he'd wanted. Hopefully, it also meant that with his help, they'd manage to disband the conclave.

It wasn't going to be easy.

"And this door isn't guarded?" Mordred asked.

"It can't be, because the conclave doesn't want anyone to know about it," Percy said. "The problem is reaching it, because the doors that lead to this one *are* guarded."

Mordred nodded while Bay leaned back in his chair. He couldn't help but smile. They were nowhere near close to getting rid of the conclave, but they were moving forward, which was all that mattered. They'd manage eventually. They were immortal, which meant they had all the time in the world to obtain what they wanted.

His phone vibrated in his pocket. He took it out, frowning when he saw Mordred's name on the screen. It was a text, so he opened it, wondering why Mordred would text him when he was on the other side of the table.

He's doing a good job.

Bay grinned. He didn't look at his best friend so no one around the table would know what they were doing. *He is. Does that mean you trust him?*

Mordred didn't answer right away, and Bay watched the three dots dance on the screen. It was a heavy question, but he knew what he'd answer if Mordred asked *him* if he trusted Percy.

I don't know. I want to, but I'm not sure we can yet, was Mordred's answer.

Bay nodded. He understood that he trusted Percy because of what they shared and because they spent a lot more time together than Percy did with anyone else in the house. Eventually, people would get used to having him around, and they'd see how important this was to him. In the meantime, Bay and Percy would be stuck together.

The meeting lasted a while longer. They went over everything Percy could give them about the conclave in the building. They were just breaking up for lunch when the alarms started blaring. Mordred swore while Percy looked at Bay with wide eyes.

"Is someone trying to enter?" he asked.

Bay shook his head. "It's not that kind of alarm. This means that someone contacted us because they need help with the conclave."

Mordred threw himself behind his desk and picked up his phone. He put it on speaker, then called the security room.

It was something they'd set up as soon as technology made it possible. That one phone number was given out by all fallen heroes and some of the supernatural creatures they helped. It was word-of-mouth, and it worked well that way. There was always someone on duty to answer the phone if it rang, and unfortunately, it had to be done often.

"Talk to me," Mordred said when someone answered.

"You should come to the conference room. I'm headed there with more info," Eudocia said.

Bay hadn't realized she was in the security room, but that was good. As one of Mordred's seconds, she knew what to do and how to do it fast.

Mordred, Bay, and Percy ran to the conference room. It wasn't originally set up as a conference room, but it was big enough to have space for all fallen heroes who lived in the house and more, so that was what they'd done with it. There were chairs, a massive table, and a screen on the wall. Fallen heroes were already streaming through the door, knowing what the alarm meant.

Once they were inside, Mordred, Bay, and Percy made a beeline for the table, where Eudocia was already working. She briefly looked at them when they arrived, but she didn't waste time saying hello.

"Two heroes were sent on a mission. I don't know all the details yet, but apparently, the conclave wanted them to execute a tribe of fauns."

Dammit. Why would the conclave want that? Fauns were nature creatures, and they wanted nothing more than to be left alone to live in the forest. "How many casualties?" he asked.

Eudocia shook her head. "None that I know of. The heroes found more resistance than they expected. One of them is wounded, while the other has a hostage. That's the problem. They're trying to leave, but of course, the fauns won't allow them to. The heroes won't let the hostage go. It's a standoff, and the fauns don't know how to solve it."

Mordred nodded. "All right. We're sending a team in, with the possibility of adding a second one if we need to. Who wants to go?" he asked, looking around the room.

To everyone's surprise, Percy's hand was one of the first to shoot in the air. Bay had expected that, but he wasn't sure they could give Percy what he wanted. They were still bound together, and while they could take off the bracelets, would anyone trust Percy enough to want that? Bay did, but he wasn't the one who'd have to make that decision.

It would be hard for Percy if Mordred said no. Percy wanted to contribute and to be part of their team, and even though he'd helped already, it wasn't enough yet. He was still being kept aside, and he wanted that to be over. Bay understood, and he wanted the same, but that didn't mean they'd obtain it. Mordred had to trust Percy a hundred per-cent before he'd allow him to go on missions, and Bay didn't think that was the case yet.

It would break Percy's heart, even though he would also understand. Still, Bay held his breath as he looked at Mor-dred, waiting for his decision. Whatever happened, it wouldn't change Bay's feelings for Percy. It might change the decision Percy had made to stay, though, and that thought was terrifying.

Percy wasn't an idiot. He knew everyone was wary of allow-ing him to go on that mission, and honestly, he was, too. It would be the first time he went out as a fallen hero and the first time he'd have to face conclave heroes as one. He didn't know who the two heroes involved here were, but they might recognize him, and he didn't know how he'd deal with that. He wouldn't find out until he had to, and he felt this was the best way to make that happen.

Bay trusted him, but Percy was pretty sure he was the only one. Mordred might be on his way to, as were Cecil and a few other people. Still, until Percy showed them he could be trusted, they wouldn't be able to move forward, which was what he wanted.

"Why are you asking?" Mordred asked, crossing his arms over his chest.

Percy had the attention of everyone in the room. As much as he disliked it, he also understood. He kept his focus on Mordred, happy to feel Bay's presence next to him. Even if Mordred said no, Percy wouldn't lose Bay. He wouldn't lose any of this. He'd just have to work harder to make everyone see he was on their side.

He cleared his throat. "Think about it. I can use my siren

ability to convince the hero to let go of hostage. Once I do, you can subdue both of them."

Mordred slowly nodded. "It does sound like a good plan. If you use your ability, no one will have to go near the hero. That means the hostage won't be in more danger."

"Exactly." Percy was happy that Mordred understood. He'd been afraid Mordred would brush him off without listening to him, but he should have known better. No matter how much he'd disliked and even hated Mordred in the beginning, he was a good person. He did this because he wanted to help people, and Percy wanted to help him make that happen.

"But I can't allow it," Mordred continued.

Percy deflated. He'd expected it, but he hoped things would go differently. "Because you don't want Bay and me to take the bracelets off."

Mordred nodded. "I want to trust you, but I'm not sure I can yet. What will happen if I let you do it and you decide to go back to the conclave?"

"I can promise you I won't, but I understand why you don't believe me."

"That's bullshit," someone in the room said.

Percy turned to see who it was, and he was stunned when Cecil pushed through the crowd to get to him. His eyes were narrow and he was clearly pissed, although Percy didn't understand at whom.

Cecil stopped in front of Mordred. "I trust Percy. He wants to help, and he should be allowed to."

"This isn't the right moment to do this," Mordred said.

"It might not be, but *when* will it be? You need Percy's help, and the only way for you to see you can trust him is to give him a chance to show you that you can."

He turned to Percy. Percy saw his lips move as he muttered something.

The bracelet on Percy's wrist went slack. Percy looked at it in shock. When he shook his hand, the bracelet slipped off and fell to the floor. Percy couldn't look away, but he had to ask why. When he peered up at Cecil, Cecil appeared satisfied. Percy opened his mouth, but nothing came out. He didn't know what to say or how to thank Cecil.

Mordred groaned. "Why did you have to do that?" He didn't sound angry, which gave Percy hope.

"Because it's the right thing to do," Cecil said. "Give him a chance. He'll surprise you." He looked around the room. "He'll surprise all of you. I know that some of the people here don't trust Percy yet. But think about how things were when you were in his place. This is an emergency, and we need Percy's ability. Do you really want the hostage to get hurt, or worse, killed, because you didn't allow Percy to help? Because I don't want that on my conscience, and I won't, now that I took the bracelets off." He turned his attention back to Mordred. "*You* will, if you order Percy to stay here."

"I'll stay with him," Bay said.

Percy wanted to ask him how he felt about them not being stuck together anymore, but now wasn't the moment. Once he would have been offended by Bay saying he would stay with him anyway, but now, he wanted Bay to.

Facing two heroes he might have worked with in the past wouldn't be easy, and Percy was very much aware of that. They'd view him as a traitor, and in a way, he was. They'd no doubt have a lot to say about that, and they wouldn't hesitate to do so. Percy would have to find a way to talk to them and convince them to let the hostage go. Maybe, if Percy was lucky, no one would be hurt. He might convince the two heroes to calm down enough so the fallen heroes could take them and portal them to the house. By the end of the day, the two heroes might be in the cell that had been Percy's home for a month.

But none of that would happen if Percy didn't go. He stood straighter. "That's fine with me. We should go, though."

Mordred sighed. "Fine. Let's go. But I'm keeping an eye on you. Bay and Cecil might trust you, but I'm not sure I do yet."

That was fine with Percy, because he hadn't expected anything different.

Mordred selected a small team, and once he had, every one of them rushed out of the room. Percy already knew they couldn't portal in or out of the house, so he wasn't surprised when he was led into the forest. He and Bay didn't have time to talk, but before they could cross the portal Mordred had opened, Bay quickly squeeze Percy's hand. They exchanged a glance, and Bay's smile told Percy everything he needed to know.

Bay trusted him, and he clearly thought Percy would do a good job. Percy hoped he wouldn't disappoint him.

He stepped through the portal, not knowing what to expect. It took him a moment to take in the situation, and when he did, he groaned.

They were in the middle of a forest, just like he'd thought. They were dealing with fauns, and that was where they lived. This forest was on a mountain, and on one side of them stood a massive stone wall.

That was where the heroes were huddled. One of them, a male, was folded on himself, holding his stomach. Percy could see blood dripping from the wound, so it had to be bad. The other hero, a female, was holding a faun around the neck. Percy had never been good at estimating age when it came to supernatural creatures, but then, it was often impossible. They weren't humans, and they didn't look or age the same way. This faun was particularly short, so it might mean a child or possibly a female.

What the faun was didn't matter. What mattered was that a conclave hero was holding them around the throat, ready to slit it if one of the people gathered around her took a step forward.

Her attention moved to the portal, and her eyes widened. It took Percy a moment to recognize her, and when he did, he knew she was angry. They'd worked together a few times, and while they weren't friends, they'd been friendly once.

"I should have known you'd betrayed us," Riva spat out.

Percy ignored the fallen heroes looking at him. He stepped forward, stopping when Riva tensed. He didn't want her to do something stupid like killing the faun. He raised his hands so she could see he wasn't armed. He was, of course, but he had nothing in his hands, and he'd try not to hurt her. He didn't want to if he didn't have to. "Hello, Riva."

"We thought you were dead."

"Well, you can see I'm not. Why don't you allow me to come closer?" Percy said, pushing his ability into his voice.

He didn't know if it would work, but he hoped so. He and Cecil had trained together, but he'd never tried it on a hero. He could too easily imagine what would happen if he failed, but he wouldn't allow it to.

He could do this. He could show Mordred and the other fallen heroes that he was on their side and that he'd be useful to their cause. He could show them he should be allowed to stay with them—and with Bay.

Bay had gone on missions with people he'd slept with before, but none had been so terrifying. He'd cared about them, but he hadn't been in love with any of them the way he was with Percy.

Bay already knew he cared about Percy, even that he was falling in love with him, but he hadn't realized just how important Percy had become to him. It was strange not to be linked to him anymore and to watch him move away more than six feet. Bay's instinct was to go after him, but he knew better. The hero Percy had called Riva looked like even the slightest thing could push her over the edge, and that was something no one wanted.

He forced himself to look away. A small group of fauns was gathered close by, several of them standing away from the group. Bay suspected the one in front was the leader of their group, and he'd be the best person to ask what had happened.

Bay stepped closer. The fauns all looked at him, but the leader stayed where he was.

"My name is Bayard," Bay said.

The leader nodded. He was short, only reaching Bay's chest. Two horns stuck up from a mop of curly dark hair, and his hairy legs were those of a goat.

"Can you tell me what happened?" Bay asked when the faun didn't introduce himself.

The faun grunted. "What do you think happened? They barged into our village and started hurting people. We attacked them, and they fled. One of them was wounded, so he couldn't open a portal. The other tried, but we were on to them. We almost caught her, but she grabbed one of us." He looked straight at Bay. "We don't care what you do with them. We just want our faun back."

Bay nodded and went back to Mordred to explain what had happened. He was curious to know how Mordred wanted to do this. When they could, they captured heroes and stuck them in the cells where Percy had spent so much time. One of the heroes in front of them needed medical attention, but Riva wouldn't allow them to move closer. That meant Percy had to do all the work, and Bay wasn't sure how that would go.

Percy was slowly moving closer to her. He was talking in a soft, gentle tone, and even though the power wasn't aimed at

Bay, he could feel it in Percy's voice. He wasn't surprised to see Riva's hand lower from the faun's neck. She didn't drop the knife she was holding, but hopefully, Percy would manage to catch it.

"That's good," Percy said. "I know you're scared, but as long as you do what I ask, everything will be okay. I want you to step away from the faun. Lower your knife. No one is going to hurt you."

Riva didn't move right away. Bay held his breath, wondering if Percy enough control over his ability to do this. He hoped that was the case, because he didn't know what they'd do if it wasn't.

But Riva finally lowered her arm and stared at Percy. It was as if she was waiting for him to give her another order, which Bay supposed was true.

The hero was behind her, still curled on himself. His eyes were wide as he stared at Percy, and Bay knew they couldn't allow either of those heroes to go back to the conclave. If they did, the conclave would know what Percy could do and what he was, and they'd come after him.

He slowly started moving toward Percy and the conclave heroes. The sooner they put handcuffs on the heroes, the better it would be for everyone. Before Bay could get close enough, though, the faun who'd been held hostage turned around and kicked Riva on the shin. She stumbled back, rapidly blinking. Then her expression shifted, and Bay knew Percy's ability wasn't working anymore.

Riva snarled. "What are you doing to me?" she looked around and seemed to realize the position she was in. She threw her hand out to create a portal. "You'll pay for this."

Instead of reaching for the other hero like Bay had expected, she snatched Percy's arm and pulled him along. Percy tried to resist, but Riva was having none of that, and she was still holding a knife. She held it up and said something Bay couldn't hear. Percy nodded, then looked back.

Percy found Bay's gaze. Bay started to move forward, not caring what would happen to him if he did. Riva could stab him for all he cared, as long as he got to Percy and managed to keep him safe.

Someone grabbed Bay's waist and pulled him back. Bay fought. He needed to get to Percy before Percy disappeared.

But he couldn't. Bay was still staring when Riva held her knife up to Percy's throat. He was still quietly talking to her, but evidently either his ability either wasn't working, or he wasn't focused enough to make it work. No matter the reason, he couldn't resist Riva, not when she was threatening him with the knife. He allowed her to pull him forward and into the portal.

He glanced back one last time. He looked sad but also not surprised, which Bay took as meaning he'd expected something like this to happen. Bay tried to fight against whoever was holding him — Constantine — but he wouldn't let go.

"I'll find you!" he yelled at Percy. "You won't be with them for long. I'll find you, and I'll bring you home."

Then Percy was gone, but that didn't mean Bay wouldn't keep his promise. He'd get Percy back if it was the last thing he did, even if he had to destroy the entire conclave and the heroes to do it. He didn't care about the casualties. He'd burn the world down if he had to.

CHAPTER ELEVEN

Percy knew he had to act fast. If he didn't, his ass would be dragged to the closest cell and he'd be executed after the conclave was done interrogating and torturing him. He wanted to think he wouldn't tell them anything about the fallen heroes, but he couldn't be sure, and he wouldn't put Bay in danger.

So as soon as he was through the portal, he punched Riva in the face. She stumbled back, but she was a hero. One punch wouldn't be enough to put her down.

Percy grabbed her arm and slammed her wrist against the wall. Her fingers opened, and the knife fell to the floor. Now that he wasn't afraid of being stabbed, Percy punched her again, then again, until she slid down. Her face was a mess of blood, and Percy's stomach churned at the thought of what he'd just done.

How was it possible that he'd easily killed supernatural creatures who hadn't deserved it, yet he wanted to throw up at the thought of rendering Riva unconscious? But that was what he needed. Luckily for him, the room in which Riva had opened the portal was empty. Someone would come soon, though, and when they did, Percy didn't want them to realize who he was and why he was here. If he managed to pass himself off as a conclave hero, he might be able to make it out before someone realized who he was and that he'd been gone for more than a month.

Riva groaned, so Percy punched her again. She stopped moving just as he heard people running toward them. He

149

picked up the knife, hid it in his jeans, then reached down and hauled Riva into his arms just as two heroes burst into the room.

Percy didn't give them time to think about what was happening. He rushed toward them, thrusting Riva into the arms of the first one. "Take her to the infirmary," he ordered.

The hero stared at him. "But you—"

Dammit. This one seemed to recognize Percy, even though Percy didn't know him. "Go. She freed me from where I was kept prisoner, but she was attacked. She needs a healer, and she needs it now."

Percy wouldn't have a lot of time to leave before she woke up, and since he was in the conclave building, he wanted to take advantage of it. He knew exactly where to go. Being a hero for three hundred years came in handy when you were looking for the offices of the conclave members so you could steal documents and plans.

The hero finally nodded and moved toward the door. Percy turned his attention to the other one. "Go with him. I want to know how she is as soon as the healers see her."

"I should raise the alarm," the hero protested.

He was young, maybe even too young to be a full-fledged hero. There was no way to know when the conclave had found him, so Percy wasn't sure if he was a hero yet or if he was still in training. Still, given how young he was, he'd probably obey Percy's orders without thinking twice about it.

Percy snorted. "What alarm? We got away. We'll have to go back to those fauns to complete the mission, since we weren't able to do it this time, but it can wait. They're not going anywhere."

The hero's eyes were wide. He nodded eagerly and rushed after the other one, leaving Percy alone. Percy waited until their footsteps faded in the distance. Then he took a deep breath and moved toward the door.

The building was like it had been the last time he'd seen it. It felt like it had been a lifetime ago instead of not even two months, but that was because Percy had changed so much. Still, he'd been a hero for close to three hundred years, so he walked down the hallways as if he belonged, with his back straight and his head held high. A few heroes he crossed paths with stared, but no one tried to stop him. Percy had made up a little story if they tried, but thankfully, he didn't have to use it.

He did once he reached the office he was looking for. He knew all the conclave members, and Hester was the one who spent less time in the building. She didn't enjoy having to work, which Percy had always disliked about her, but in this case, it played in his favor. If he managed to get into that office and to the computer, he could get everything the fallen heroes needed.

First, he'd have to convince Hester's assistant she was needed somewhere else.

He walked in, still acting as if he was supposed to be there. The hero in training behind the desk looked up at him, blinking. She got to her feet, and Percy smiled. He pushed his ability toward the front of his mind, weaving it into his words. "Hello. Hester is expecting me," he said.

The hero in training frowned. "But she's not here."

"She is. You just saw her walk past you half an hour ago. She told you she had an important meeting and that you shouldn't bother her. She also said you couldn't mention it to anyone and that she trusts you. You should go get something to eat in the meantime."

The hero in training blinked, and Percy prayed this would work. He'd been training with Cecil to control his ability, but he still didn't have a good handle on it. Hopefully, the fact that the personal assistant was still in training would help. She wasn't fighting Percy's ability as far as he could feel, which was a relief.

She slowly nodded. "Hester is waiting for you," she said.

Percy smiled at her. "Thank you. Oh, one last thing. You won't remember any of this by the time you're done eating." He pushed as much of his ability as he could into those words. Nothing would happen if the conclave found out he'd been here as long as he left before they did so, but just in case, he didn't want the personal assistant to be able to describe him.

He waited where he was and watched her move toward the door. Once she'd left, he rushed to it, locking it before going into Hester's office.

He'd never been here, but word among the heroes was that all the offices for the conclave members looked like each other. He'd seen others, and he knew there was a hidden door in the wall so Hester could run away if she had to do. He locked that one, too. Then he sat behind the desk. He dug into one of the drawers, looking for a USB drive. Once he had one, he turned the computer on and prayed he'd be able to access the databases.

When he'd disappeared, his access to the database had been revoked. It meant he wouldn't be able to give his jailers any information they shouldn't have, and Percy wasn't surprised to see that entering his name and password didn't work. Luckily for him, he'd been with the conclave long enough to know the password of at least one conclave member.

He'd never done anything with it. Hell, he'd done his best to forget it, but it was seared in his brain. Accessing the computer with those credentials would be even better than using his because it meant he'd have access to more info.

Some conclave members were getting too complacent and thought nothing could happen to them. Percy would show them otherwise.

He quickly clicked through the database, sending

everything he thought could be useful to the drive he'd stuck into the computer. There was a list of supernatural creatures, both the ones the conclave had gotten rid of and the ones they were keeping an eye on. Percy made sure to copy that to the drive, then lists of heroes and missions, both old and planned ones. He found the file of the mission during which he'd been captured, and the one from today with the fauns. Just in case, he quickly typed a fake report. It wouldn't do much, but it might give him enough time to flee from the building.

That was all he wanted. This was madness, and it hadn't been planned, but he was taking advantage of the situation. He might not make it out of here, but he sure was going to try.

For the first time, he had something to go back to. He hoped Bay knew he *was* coming back, or that at the very least, he was trying. He didn't know what he'd do if Bay lost faith in him, but he'd do everything he could to find out if he had or if he still trusted him.

Percy never came back. Bay stared at the space where the hero had opened that portal for way too long. He expected another portal to open and Percy to stumble through, but it didn't happen.

Things around him were moving, though. The fallen heroes had stepped in so the fauns wouldn't kill the wounded conclave hero, who was still leaning heavily against the side of the mountain. He was trying to defend himself, but he was weak from blood loss. He might not die from this, but that didn't mean he didn't feel it. Constantine, who was one of the fallen heroes Mordred had decided to take with him, rolled his eyes and punched the hero in the face. The hero slumped against the side of the mountain, and Constantine moved in, restraining him. Once he finished, other fallen heroes rushed to help. One of them opened a portal, and together, they walked the hero through. He'd need to see a healer, and someone would take care of him at the house.

But Bay couldn't go yet. He had to stay and make sure Percy was okay, but how was he supposed to do that? He'd hoped Percy would come back right away, but what if more heroes had been waiting for him? Bay remembered the room where the heroes opened the portals. It was usually empty, because it was never good when a portal opened where you were standing, but that didn't mean someone hadn't been there.

Or maybe Percy hadn't been able to subdue Riva. Maybe she'd kicked his ass, and he was being dragged into one of the cells in the conclave building right now.

"Do you think he'll come back?" Mordred asked.

Mordred wasn't afraid that something had happened to Percy the way Bay was. He was asking if Percy had been lying to them the entire time and had always been on the conclave's side.

Bay opened his mouth to snap at his best friend, but before he could, Cecil intervened. "Don't be an idiot. If he can, he'll come back."

Mordred arched a brow, but thankfully, he wasn't easily offended. "You sound sure of that, but Percy was a conclave hero only a few months ago. What's to say he hasn't gone back to them and is telling them everything he saw in the house?"

Cecil put his hands on his hips and glared. "You haven't spent a lot of time with him. You were eager to use him for his knowledge, but do you actually know him? Because I do. I've helped him train his ability. I spent time talking to him. I don't know what happened when he crossed the portal, but if he's not coming back, it's not because he's not planning to."

"He might have been captured," Bay said.

"Maybe, but he also might have decided to take advantage of this," Cecil said, his tone more reassuring. "Have faith in him."

"I do. But what if he's hurt? What if he can't come back?"

"Then we'll *get* him back," Mordred intervened, surprising Bay.

"You were just saying you thought he'd gone back to the conclave," he pointed out.

"I don't know what to believe or if I can trust him, but you and Cecil do. That's enough for me to believe he's planning on coming back and isn't doing so because of a very good reason." Mordred looked around. "But we have to be ready in case we have to go get him. That means cleaning up the situation here as well as we can before that happens."

Bay sighed. He knew what cleaning up meant in this case. They had to make sure none of the fauns had been hurt, and if they had, they'd offer them a healer. If the fauns were okay, they'd still have to talk to them just to touch base and ask what had happened. Usually, it was the part of the job Bay preferred, because it meant the danger was gone and everyone was okay, but today, he couldn't stop thinking about Percy.

Bay realized how easy it would be for Percy to tell the conclave everything he'd learned. Even Percy had admitted it would be easier for him to go back to the conclave and ignore his siren half again. He didn't want to do that, though, and Bay had to keep that in mind. He had to remember that Percy had changed over the past few months. He was still hesitant and worried, but he'd left the conclave behind, and he wasn't going back.

But it would be just like him to make the most of the situation he was in. He wanted to prove himself to the fallen heroes and Mordred, and he was in the conclave building right now. That meant he had access to information they wouldn't be able to reach otherwise, not unless Mordred's secret contact in the conclave obtained it for them, but they couldn't. That would expose whoever it was, and the fallen heroes needed that person to stay where they were.

That meant that if they wanted that information, they had to get someone into the conclave building — and they just had. There was no way Riva had taken Percy anywhere else. She'd been outraged and had recognized him, so she'd want to take him to the conclave to have him punished. Hopefully, Percy had found a way around that.

Bay had to keep up hope that Percy was coming back. It wasn't just because the conclave wouldn't accept him and his siren half, or because he believed in what the fallen heroes were doing. All of that did matter, but what mattered the most to Bay was what he and Percy had. There was no way Percy was giving that up, and that was one thing Bay was sure of. It didn't matter that Mordred wasn't convinced or that Bay could feel the pitying gazes of his friends watching him.

He truly believed in Percy, and nothing was changing his mind on that.

Percy peeked out the door, hoping the hero in training hadn't come back. She wasn't anywhere to be seen, so he slipped out, locked the door again, and moved on to the next one.

That was where things got dicey. A hero was walking down the hallway, and he stumbled on Percy just as Percy closed the second door. The hero looked from Percy to the door, and his eyes narrowed. Percy didn't want to hurt him or anyone he didn't have to hurt, but he readied himself. This wasn't going to be pretty, but he wasn't letting anyone keep him from Bay and from getting the information he'd stolen back to the fallen heroes.

"Who are you?" the hero asked.

At least he hadn't recognized Percy. "None of your business."

"I think it's my business when I saw you coming out of an office I know is empty. The conclave leader isn't there."

"I'm aware of that. Her assistant just told me. Do you have any more questions for me, or can I go to work?"

Hopefully, the hero would think Percy had every right to be here and that he'd been trying to find Hester. Percy had admitted to that, and the hero didn't have a reason to doubt him. Percy didn't have a lot of time, though. Riva would be awake soon, and she'd sound the alarm. Percy had to be out of here before that happened or he'd be in trouble.

"I think you should come with me," the hero said.

Percy sighed. He didn't want to use his ability, because it would tell the heroes he used it on what he was, but he didn't have a choice.

He pushed it to the front and smiled at the hero. "I don't have to come with you," he said. "There's no reason for me to. I was only looking for Hester, and you told me she wasn't here. You're going back to work, and so am I. You won't remember seeing me here. It's not important."

The hero nodded. He kept staring at Percy until Percy realized why he wasn't moving.

"You should go get something to eat now," Percy said. "You're hungry."

The hero finally moved. Percy watched until the hero disappeared around the corner. Then he turned around and froze.

A man was standing in the middle of the hallway, staring at him. He looked young, barely in his early twenties, but Percy knew him to be much older. His dark hair flopped over his forehead, and, along with his clear gray eyes, it made him look even younger. He also appeared harmless, but no one could be a hero and harmless. No, this man was dangerous, even though he was young and slight and looked like he wouldn't be able to fight his way out of a wet paper bag.

Percy knew that man. He'd recognize every single conclave member anywhere, and Micah was one.

And he'd seen what Percy had just done.

Percy swallowed. There had to be a reason Micah hadn't raised the alarm yet and was still staring at Percy. He was one of the nicest conclave members, but Percy didn't know him well. He didn't know any conclave member well because they kept themselves apart. Still, Micah was part of the conclave, which meant he was Percy's enemy.

Percy straightened and opened his mouth, but Micah raised a hand. "Don't try to lure me, please," he said.

He didn't sound angry or scared, which puzzled Percy even more. "You're a conclave member," he said.

Micah nodded. "I'm aware of that." He looked around. "You need to get out of here before someone realizes who you are. Come on. I'll walk you to the portal room."

"Why?"

Micah looked torn. Percy understood he might not be willing to tell him anything. It was how things worked with the heroes. Still, he wanted an explanation and to be sure he wasn't walking into a trap.

"I suppose it'll come out soon anyway," Micah muttered before looking right and left. The hallway was empty, and Micah looked satisfied. "I work with your friends."

Percy frowned. "My friends?"

"Mordred contacted me a few minutes ago. He told me you were here in the building and to find you."

Percy gaped. Micah was a conclave member, yet he was in contact with Mordred? That meant Mordred had a spy right in the conclave, and he hadn't told Percy. It made sense that he hadn't, since he wasn't sure he could trust Percy, but Percy would have appreciated the warning.

Micah gestured, and this time, Percy followed him. He had a dozen questions, but he was pretty sure he wasn't supposed to ask them. If he was lucky, Micah would answer, so he might as well ask.

"So you work with Mordred?" he asked as they walked down the hallway.

They were going fast, but not so fast that anyone they crossed paths with would think something was wrong.

Micah nodded. "We were heroes together. We never lost contact, and since I'm investigating the conclave with a small group of heroes and former conclave members, it made sense to work with him."

"You're investigating the conclave?"

"I have been for a while now, but it's not easy. Most conclave members are wary of everyone, including the rest of the conclave. They know that what they're doing is wrong."

"Yet you're letting them do it anyway."

"I wish I could do more, but for now, the only thing we can do is investigate them. I need proof of what they've been doing. I have to be able to arrest them and show the heroes I was right to do that. There'll be a trial, and they should be convicted for what they've done."

"And you're also helping the fallen heroes. You have to be the one who tells Mordred about the missions."

The corner of Micah's lips curled. "I am when I'm able. I'm not the only one here who works with the fallen heroes, as you call them. I'm also not the only one who thinks that what the conclave is doing is wrong. I wish I could do more, but we're a minority."

But they were working against the conclave, and Micah was obviously on the right side of things. Percy wished he'd known about this sooner, but he supposed now was better than never. "I stole everything I could from Hester's computer," he said.

To his surprise, Micah laughed. "So you went straight to her, huh?"

"I knew she wouldn't be in her office."

"You were right, and please, give everything you got to Mordred. I don't think he ever told anyone about me, not even his seconds, so you should probably talk to him about that before you do."

So that was why Bay hadn't mentioned anything. It had hurt Percy to think that maybe he didn't trust him entirely, but it looked like Bay didn't know, either. It would be fun to watch Mordred having to tell both Bay and Eudocia.

They reached the portal room. Micah's expression and stance changed. He'd been careful before, but he'd been friendly. Now, he looked every bit like the conclave member he was.

He strode inside, eyed the blood on the floor, and arched a brow at Percy. Percy shrugged. Micah would find out what happened here soon enough, and he didn't need Percy to let him know.

They weren't alone in the room, and Micah turned his attention to the two heroes standing there. "What are you doing here?"

"Only half of the team we sent out to the fauns came back. Riva wasn't alone, and we're looking for that other person."

Micah nodded curtly. "I see." He threw his hand out to create a portal.

One of the heroes took a step forward, maybe to stop him, or at the very least, to ask him what he was doing, but one glare from Micah was enough to make him stop. The hero took a step back and leaned toward the other, who shook his head.

Once the portal had been created, Percy moved to it. His heart raced and he still expected something to happen and someone to stop him, so he wasn't surprised when Micah leaned closer, putting a hand on his wrist.

Percy froze and waited.

"This is an untraceable portal," Micah murmured.

Percy was impressed. He hadn't thought the conclave members knew how to create untraceable portals, but he'd heard about it from one of the fallen heroes. He wanted to learn how to create them, but he hadn't found the opportunity so far.

"I'm sending you to the fauns in case Mordred left someone there. Say hi to him for me, will you? And tell him to make good use of the information you stole."

Percy nodded. He wanted to ask his questions, but he couldn't afford to stay. He strode through the portal without glancing back. Hopefully, Micah wouldn't get in trouble over what he'd just done, but if he did, Mordred would step in and save him. No matter how grumpy Mordred was, no matter that he didn't trust Percy, he was still a good person, and Percy knew he'd made the right choice.

He was a fallen hero now, and he wouldn't change that for anything.

Bay had decided to stay with the faun tribe in case this was where Percy opened his portal to come back to him. He didn't know if that would be the case or if Percy would go back to the house directly, but he knew his man. Percy wouldn't want to put the other fallen heroes or the house in danger, so if he had to portal away from the conclave, he'd do it in a place that wouldn't get their attention. Besides, Percy knew that Haven could create untraceable portals. He'd probably portal here, then contact Bay so they could get an untraceable portal to the house.

So Bay waited, right where Percy had disappeared through that portal earlier. Mordred had wanted to leave a few other fallen heroes with him, but Bay had refused. He didn't need someone to hold his hand. He knew Percy was coming back.

He just didn't know when and where.

He could hear the fauns close by, having a party. They were celebrating how the day had gone by drinking and dancing. They'd asked Bay if he wanted to join them, but he'd refused. Right now, he didn't feel like celebrating. Besides, fauns could drink anyone under the table, and Bay didn't want to wake up with a headache tomorrow.

Instead of partying with the fauns, Bay sat against the stone wall of the mountain and tilted his head to look at the sky. The stars were the same ones he could see at the house, but they felt different. Maybe it was because he was alone now. Percy had only been in his life for a little under two months, but he was already part of it, and Bay couldn't imagine being without him.

What if he wasn't coming back? Percy would if he could, but he'd portaled to the conclave with a hero. What if she'd subdued him? What if the conclave had captured Percy and he couldn't come back?

But no. Mordred had taken Bay aside to tell him his contact inside the conclave had promised he'd find Percy and set him free. It might take a little time, but Percy would be back with Bay soon, and they'd go home. That was all Bay wanted.

Well, that, and for the conclave to be destroyed. If they as much as touched a hair on Percy's head, Bay would be the one to destroy them, member by member.

A shimmer at the corner of his eye caught his attention. He turned and scrambled to his feet as he watched the portal growing bigger. He couldn't look away, not even when no one came through. He waited, the seconds ticking by. He was ready to defend himself and the fauns if he had to, but he hoped it was Percy.

"Are they attacking us again?" someone asked.

Bay jumped and glared at the faun. "They're not. It's a fallen hero, so you can go back to your party." He was pretty sure this faun was the one who'd been taken hostage. He still didn't know if it was a female or child, or just very short for a faun, but he wasn't about to ask.

The faun's eyes narrowed. "Are you sure?"

Their voice slurred slightly, which wasn't surprising considering the fauns had been celebrating for hours. Bay would be surprised if they still had wine left.

"I'm sure," he confirmed just as Percy came through the portal.

Bay's knees almost buckled in relief. He left the faun behind, not caring if he was rude. Percy was looking around, tense and ready to attack. He almost did when he heard Bay, but he realized who Bay was at the last moment. Bay should have lit a fire or something like that to make sure there was enough light in the darkness of the night for Percy to identify him, but he hadn't thought about it. That didn't matter now, because as soon as he was close enough, Percy's shoulders relaxed, and he smiled.

Bay grabbed Percy and pulled him into his arms. Percy came willingly, wrapping himself around Bay, and they stood there as the portal slowly vanished behind them. They needed to move, but first, Bay wanted to reassure himself that Percy was okay.

He leaned back, looking at him. He didn't look hurt as far as Bay could see. "Are you okay?" Bay asked.

Percy nodded and looked around. "Has everyone gone home?"

"They have, but we weren't sure if you'd portal here or there, so I decided to stay."

Percy snorted. "They really don't trust me, do they? I'd never portal to the house. I wouldn't put its location in danger that way." He paused. "Besides, I wasn't the one who opened this portal. Mordred's contact in the conclave did. It's not traceable, so we don't have to be worried, but I still want to go home as soon as possible."

Bay had never asked too many questions about Mordred's contact in the conclave, but now, he would. He understood why Mordred had kept it to himself. The fewer people who knew about them, the safer the contact was. But Mordred could trust Bay, and the time had come for him and Eudocia to know more about it. They weren't just fallen heroes. They were Mordred's seconds, and they were right there with him in his plans to defeat the conclave.

But first, Bay would take Percy home.

He put his hand out and created a portal. Percy didn't hesitate, and they walked through it hand in hand. Bay didn't want to let Percy go. He knew it was stupid, but he felt like Percy would disappear again if he did, and it wasn't something he was prepared to face.

"How did you make it out?" he asked once they were in the forest behind the house. It would take them a little while to get to the house, and while Bay should probably call Mordred to tell him what happened, he wanted to be with Percy more. Mordred would understand.

"I punched Riva unconscious as soon as we were out of the portal before she could call for help. A few heroes arrived, but I told them we'd been sent on a mission, and since she was unconscious, she couldn't confirm or deny it. I told them to take her to the infirmary. Then I headed to an office that belongs to one of the conclave members. I knew she wouldn't be in because she never is."

"Hester."

"I didn't realize she'd been a conclave member for so long."

"She hasn't, but we know about her and how she dislikes work." Which, in this case, had been positive, at least for Percy.

Percy nodded. "I convinced her personal assistant to go get

some food and broke into her office. I copied everything I could from her computer. I think Mordred will be happy about it."

"How do you know her password?"

"Not hers."

Bay was curious. "Whose password do you know, then? You don't have to tell me if you don't want to, but I'm curious."

"Kalliope. She's kind of a mess with passwords and technology, so sometimes she needs help with them. I happened to be there one day. I still remember the password, even though I probably shouldn't."

He was right about that, but maybe, deep inside, he'd already realized back then that he might need it one day. Bay wouldn't have cared if Percy had come back empty-handed, but this way, they had one more opportunity to win their fight against the conclave.

"I also met Mordred's conclave contact," Percy continued.

"Who is it?"

Percy looked amused. "Do you think I should tell you? Mordred hasn't for now."

"But he's going to, because I won't take no for an answer anymore." They were stepping into the thick of the fight against the conclave, and it was time.

Bay looked at the house. They were almost at the door, and in only a few moments, they'd be inside and everyone would gather around them. Before they did, he wanted to talk to Percy.

Bay stopped a little away from the door. Since he was holding Percy's hand, Percy stopped, too. Now that they weren't in danger anymore, Bay took a moment to kiss him.

Percy sighed and pressed closer to Bay. "This is nice," he murmured.

"It is." Bay's voice sounded strangled as if he was having

trouble speaking, and he was. He wanted to say so many things, and he didn't know how to say them. Perhaps the easiest way would be just to do it. "I love you."

Percy's eyes widened. "You do?"

"I already told you I was falling in love with you. Why are you so surprised?"

"Because it's only been a few weeks."

"It's been nearly two months."

"And for the first month, I was locked in my cell."

Bay shook his head. "It doesn't matter how long it's been. Just because I'm immortal doesn't mean it takes me a long time to do things and to fall in love."

"You make it sound like you've fallen in love lots of times," Percy said with a huff.

Bay kissed him again. "I haven't. You're the first person I've fallen for in hundreds of years. Considering what could happen in the near future, I wanted you to know how important you are to me. I never even considered that you might not come back. I knew you would, and if you hadn't, well, I would have come to you."

Percy already knew that, but it was good to hear. He hadn't expected Bay to declare himself tonight, and he wasn't quite sure what to say except for one thing.

"I would have done anything I had to do to come back to you," he murmured. He'd never said the next words to anyone, and the thought of doing it now was scary, but he trusted Bay more than he'd ever trusted anyone else. "And I love you, too."

Bay's lips quirked. "I thought it was too soon?"

Percy laughed, feeling lighter than he ever had. He poked Bay in the side, grinning when Bay wiggled away from his touch. "It is, but I don't think it matters. No one will care that we're in love. The only people it matters to are the two of us, and *I* don't care that it's only been two months. I know how I feel."

Bay nodded. "I do, too. And I'm glad you came back."

Percy would have found a way even if he'd been captured. He was relieved he hadn't had to fight his way out of the conclave building, if anything because it meant he'd be of use to the fallen heroes now. He didn't know what Mordred had planned or what would happen, but he'd be there right next to Bay when they finally made their move.

Unfortunately, they couldn't linger outside for too long. Just like Percy had thought, as soon as they were inside the house, they were swarmed by people. It was almost like they'd been waiting right by the door — they probably were. Percy was stunned by everyone's reaction, especially when they seemed to be happy to see him.

Had they been worried?

Constantine patted Percy's back so hard that Percy stumbled. "We wouldn't have left you in their hands," he said. "We'd have stormed the conclave building to get you out."

"Thank you." What else was Percy supposed to say?

"Now that you've seen he's okay, maybe you could allow me to talk to him?" Mordred asked from the other side of the entrance.

His words were enough for the heroes to scatter. A few patted Percy's back or his arm as they walked past, leaving him stunned. He watched as they streamed into the various hallways and rooms that opened on the entrance, then finally turned his attention to Mordred.

The man was standing there, dressed all in black and looking fierce. Percy hesitated, wondering if Mordred would believe he'd managed to get out of the conclave building on his own or if maybe he thought the conclave knew about it and was sending Percy back to spy.

Percy swallowed when Mordred walked closer. He kept his focus on Mordred's face, which was why it took him a moment to see that Mordred was offering him his hand to shake. Percy blinked at it, then took it, wondering what was going on.

"I'm glad to see you home," Mordred said.

The words shouldn't have made Percy feel like he was choking. "I'm glad to be home," he murmured.

"Are you hurt? Do you need the infirmary?"

"I'm fine. Not even a scratch or a bruise."

Mordred stared at Percy for a moment before nodding. "Good. We should go to my office to talk about what happened."

The only thing Percy wanted to do was to go to his and Bay's bedroom and not come out until tomorrow, but he knew better. Mordred needed to know everything that happened, and Percy wanted to give him the USB drive that contained the information he'd stolen. As soon as this was over, though, he was dragging Bay to their room.

They followed Mordred to his office. Percy was curious, so he asked, "What happened to the hero who was wounded?"

"We got him to the infirmary. He's still there, but as soon as the healers say he's okay to be moved, he'll go to your cell."

Percy couldn't help but smile. "It's not really my cell anymore, is it?"

"I suppose it's not. Hopefully, he won't have to stay there as long as you did."

"Do you know anything about him?" Percy hadn't recognized him, but that didn't mean anything. The conclave tended to pair differently every time so they wouldn't become friends, but Percy still didn't know all of them.

"His name is Clifford. He's not very old, just a few decades. I hope it means it'll be easier to convince him of what the conclave really is. I'm surprised the conclave thought he was a good fit to attack a tribe of fauns."

"They underestimate supernatural creatures every day," Percy said. He had, too, until Bay had opened his eyes to the truth.

"Maybe you can talk to him once he's better. You were in his place only a few months ago. You might be able to connect with him through that."

"I'll be happy to do it, if you think that's appropriate."

Mordred looked amused. "I would never have thought those words would come out of your mouth two months ago."

"And you would have been wrong."

They reached Mordred's office. Percy wasn't surprised to see several people in it already, and he smiled at all of them. Thor and Cecil were there, along with Isaac, Tryg, Haven, Dimitri, Amyas, and Eudocia. Percy was happy to see all of them, which still stunned him. Five of those people were supernatural creatures. One was a human who was now immortal. Two were fallen heroes.

Yet they were Percy's family.

They gathered around him, happy to see him except for Tryg, but then, he never seemed happy to see anyone. Isaac even hugged Percy, which earned them a glare from Tryg. He didn't try to intervene. He never did, no matter how anxious he was about Isaac's safety. He always allowed him to make his own decisions.

Once Percy was free of hugs and had reassured everyone he was fine, he dug into his pocket and took out the USB drive. He held it out to Mordred, who took it without question.

"This is with the compliments of Hester," he said. "And Kalliope."

"You're going to have to explain."

Percy flopped into one of the chairs. He was exhausted, but

he had to go through this before he could finally get some rest. "That's all the information I managed to steal about supernatural creatures, past and future missions, and all the heroes who currently work for the conclave."

Now that he'd dropped the bomb, he leaned back and watched the reactions. He was happy to be home, and even happier to be here with something that would help the fallen heroes in their fight against the conclave. He suspected not a lot of people in this room had believed he'd come back, but he had, and he'd continue coming back until they all trusted him.

Bay couldn't stop smiling. Percy had dropped a bomb, and it was fun to watch everyone react to it.

"How did you do that?" Eudocia asked.

"I knew Hester wouldn't be in her office, so I went straight there as soon as I could," Percy answered.

"But you went through the portal with that hero. We saw you," Cecil said.

"I knocked her lights out before anyone could realize what was happening. She wasn't able to tell anyone who I was, which meant I was free to go around the building as if I belonged there."

And he had for a long time, but not anymore.

Bay sat in the chair next to Percy's and took one of his hands. Percy gave him a tiny smile, and Bay was relieved he wasn't pulling away. He didn't know how comfortable Percy was with this kind of gesture in front of their family and friends, but he seemed to be okay. Bay had been terrified he'd never see Percy again, not because Percy wouldn't come back, but because he might not be able to. Now that he had him, he was never letting him out of his sight.

"Everyone knows Hester is never in her office," Percy

continued. "And I had the password of another conclave member. Using my ability, it was fairly easy to convince Hester's personal assistant that I was supposed to be there and that she should leave. Once she did, I used Hester's computer and copied everything I could on that key." Percy looked at Mordred. "I also met your contact in the conclave. He says hi."

Mordred chuckled. "I texted him as soon as you disappeared through that portal. I hoped he could find you before you were thrown into a cell, and if he couldn't, that he could get you out."

"He did. When I left Hester's office, a hero saw me. I used my ability on him, and I didn't notice M—your contact was standing there. I was lucky it was him."

Bay cleared his throat. "By the way. Maybe it's time to tell us about your contact," he told Mordred. "You trust everyone in this room. None of us will do anything with that knowledge, not beyond what we're supposed to do with it."

Mordred sighed and sat on the corner of his desk. "I probably should have told you sooner, at the very least, when it comes to you and Eudocia. But Micah and I agreed that the fewer people knew about this, the better it would be."

"Micah?" Eudocia asked. "Do you mean the conclave member?"

"I do."

"You have a conclave member in your pocket and you didn't tell us?" Thor asked. He grinned. "I never expected that from you, Mordred."

Mordred rolled his eyes. "I don't have him in my pocket. He was the one who contacted me several hundred years ago. We were heroes together, and while I left, he never did. He became a conclave member instead. He's always been a good person, and when he realized what the other conclave members were doing, he knew something had to be done. Alone against all of them, he wouldn't have been able to do anything."

"But with your help, he might," Bay said.

"Exactly. It hasn't been easy, because he wants to do this the right way. He wants to have a trial so that every hero can find out what the conclave has been doing. It's how heroes do things, and I understand why he wants to stick with tradition, but I'm not sure it can work. Either way, we still have the same goal, and we've been working together to save as many supernatural creatures as we can and convert as many heroes as possible."

"And he couldn't steal the data because someone would have realized it was him," Percy said slowly. "That means he couldn't use it in the trial, but now, he can."

Mordred nodded. "He'll be over the moon happy with that news."

"I told him what I did when he told me you'd sent him. He knows what I stole."

"Then he's probably already planning his next step."

Their goal was finally in reach. Thanks to Percy, they might be able to put an end to the conclave as it was soon. It would probably take weeks, if not months, but they were much closer than they'd been a few hours ago. The fight might finally have an end in sight, and Bay knew everyone in the room was as excited as he was about it.

It would take work, but they had all the information they needed about the conclave, and they were working with a conclave member. For the first time, Bay finally believed they had a chance. He didn't care how long it would take. They would do this, and they would do it together.

EPILOGUE

Percy flopped onto his back. He was dying, wasn't he? It certainly felt like he was. He sucked in a breath, then another, and he relaxed as it became easier.

"You killed me," Bay groaned from the other side of the bed.

"I could say the same. I can't breathe."

Bay grinned and offered Percy his hand. Percy eagerly took it, wanting to be connected to Bay. They'd been very much connected until a few seconds ago, but this was a different kind of touch. The sex was incredible, but Percy lived for moments like these when both of them were quiet and holding hands and just being together. He'd never had this before, but now, he did, and he still had a hard time believing it.

Things were slowly changing. The conclave was still in place, and the fallen heroes were still trying to find a way to topple them. Micah was working behind the scenes, and while it was taking time, the information Percy had stolen had been useful. Micah and Mordred were spreading it slowly, only to the heroes they knew would make good use of it for now, but eventually, to all of them. Then it would be time for the trial.

The conclave wouldn't go easily. They'd been in it for too long, and they loved the power it gave them too much. Besides, it wasn't possible to get rid of the conclave entirely. It was still needed to protect humanity and the supernatural creatures who wanted nothing more than to live in peace. That was what Mordred and Micah were aiming for. They wanted to transform the conclave so the heroes who worked for it would protect everyone who needed protecting.

Hell, Mordred had mentioned something about supernatural creatures working for the conclave alongside heroes, and while Percy would have thought it impossible a few months ago, now, he kind of liked the idea. He'd been working with Cecil to control his ability, and he'd seen Thor, Tryg, and the others work with Mordred. Even though they were supernatural creatures, they were part of their fallen heroes' family, and Percy wouldn't have it any other way.

Things had changed so much in so little time, and sometimes, it made his head spin. He only had to find Bay for that to stop, though. Bay was Percy's rock in the storm, his light in the darkness, always there for him when he needed him, whatever he needed him for.

Bay's phone vibrated on his nightstand. Bay glared at it, but he didn't move to pick it up, so Percy did. He rolled on top of Bay and snatched the phone, looking down at the screen. "It's Mordred."

"What does he want?"

Percy took a moment to read the text. "He's organized a conference call with Micah. Maybe something happened? Anyway, he wants us to be there, along with the others."

Bay huffed. "I thought we wouldn't have to work today."

"I suppose I can tell him you don't want to go and that you'd rather stay in bed with me."

Bay poked Percy in the side, making him laugh. "I'd tell him, but he already knows," he said.

"I texted back that we'll be there."

They had to be. No matter how badly Percy didn't want to go head-to-head with the conclave and the heroes who still worked for them, it was necessary. He wasn't looking forward to it, and he wasn't happy about it, but Bay was right there in the middle of the fight, which meant Percy was, too.

Besides, with his ability, he could be of help. His presence might make a difference, especially with the number of heroes who would attack them. If Percy could convince them to go lock themselves in a cell or something like that, he could save a lot of lives, which was all he wanted. He was done killing people who didn't deserve it.

Some might think that the heroes still working for the conclave and obeying their orders deserved to die, but Percy didn't. He'd been one of them until recently, and he knew how hard it could be to see the truth and accept it. He had, but he'd had a lot of help from Bay and the others. He wanted to do the same with the heroes still in the dark.

He rolled back to his side of the bed. "We should get up and shower."

Bay shook his head and buried his face against Percy's neck. "I don't want to."

"I don't think Mordred will care. Besides, I want to make sure Micah is okay."

Percy was the only one who'd been in direct contact with Micah recently, and while they didn't know each other and had never been friends, he was worried about the man. Now that he knew everything Micah had done and all the ways he was working against the conclave, Percy wanted to make sure he was okay. Unfortunately, there was no way to do that. They had to wait for Micah to contact them, and he couldn't do so often, which meant they were left waiting and praying nothing had happened to him.

But they had a plan. They had allies. They were working to defeat the conclave and finally make it what it had been created for. They would expose the truth of what had been happening for too long. By the time all of this was over, the conclave would still be standing, but its members would be new, probably a mix of heroes and supernatural creatures. It would be a huge change, both for heroes and the entire supernatural world.

It was a change Percy couldn't wait to see.

About the Author

Catherine is the creator of several series, most of them paranormal, including the Whitedell Pride Series and the Gillham Pack Series. While she graduated in translation, she decided to go the writer's way because it was more fun to create her own stories and characters.

She's been living in Italy for more than twenty years, but she's a daughter of the North—Belgium to be precise—and she misses it so much that she's already planning to move back.

She loves pizza—probably too much—her son, her pets, and of course, books. She sneaks some reading time into her schedule every time she has five minutes free from writing, demands from her various pets and son, and lastly, housework.

Connect with her:

lievens.catherine@gmail.com
BookBub: https://www.bookbub.com/authors/catherine-lievens
Website: https://authorcatherinelievens.com/
Facebook: https://www.facebook.com/catherine.lievens.9
Facebook Group: https://www.facebook.com/groups/411788002341528/
Twitter: https://twitter.com/authorCLievens
Newsletter: http://eepurl.com/c-uvKn